HIS NAME IS JOHN T. BOOKER.

HE DOESN'T LIKE TO KILL—UNLESS HE HAS TO.

HE HAS TO.

They used to call Booker a hero—until they couldn't use heroes anymore.

He used to call himself a good soldier—willing to follow orders whatever they were.

But now orders were out to eliminate Booker and the men whose lives depended on him— and suddenly Booker was fighting a new kind of war, with all America turned into a free-fire zone where there was no place to hide, and so many different ways to kill or die. . . .

"GOOD GUYS WEAR BLACK"

Other SIGNET Movie Tie-ins

"GOOD GUYS WEAR BLACK"

by
Max Franklin

FROM THE SCREENPLAY BY
Mark Medoff
AND
Bruce Cohn

A SIGNET BOOK
NEW AMERICAN LIBRARY
TIMES MIRROR

Copyright © 1978 by Antares Books, Inc.

SIGNET TRADEMARK REG. U.S. PAT. OFF. AND FOREIGN COUNTRIES
REGISTERED TRADEMARK—MARCA REGISTRADA
HECHO EN CHICAGO, U.S.A.

SIGNET, SIGNET CLASSICS, MENTOR, PLUME AND MERIDIAN BOOKS
are published by The New American Library, Inc.,
1301 Avenue of the Americas, New York, New York 10019

First Printing, March, 1978

1 2 3 4 5 6 7 8 9

PRINTED IN THE UNITED STATES OF AMERICA

1

Murray Saunders sat in a hotel room in Paris, doing three things at once. He was partially singing and partially humming a mixture of two different songs with the same tune, he was smoking a thin black cigar, and he was watching a television newscast.

A tall, lean black man of about thirty with a handsome but cynical face, his voice was designed only for the shower stall. In a cracked baritone he sang, "Hurray for the red, white, and blue, for a duck may be somebody's mother—" then switched to humming because he could stand only so much of his own voice.

On the TV screen some silent black-and-white newsreel footage of American prisoners of war marching in a shabby parade along a Hanoi street was being shown. It was a typical propaganda film such as the North Vietnamese periodically released to show the world how they were winning the war. The marching prisoners, some wearing bandages, were dirty, exhausted, dispirited, and out of step, shuffling along with hanging heads and eyes glazed with battle fatigue.

Saunders stopped humming in order to listen when the scene was replaced by a newscaster seated at a desk, the picture now in color. In French the newscaster said:

*One of the biggest problems to be solved in
the peace talks is the release of prisoners such
as these Americans who have been captured
during the ten years of fighting. But the chief
American delegate, Mr. Conrad Morgan, feels
a solution is near.*

The camera cut to a closeup of the chief American delegate, a handsome, debonair man of about
thirty, surrounded by reporters who were thrusting
microphones at him. Both he and the reporters spoke
in English, and their words appeared translated into
French along the bottom of the screen. Morgan
said:

*I now sincerely believe that the North Viet-
namese delegates are dealing in good faith, and
that significant progress can now be made.*

Spotting a variety of liquor bottles, mixes, and a
bucket of ice on a table in one corner, Saunders got
up to mix himself a drink as one of the reporters
pushed a hand microphone in front of Conrad Morgan's face and asked:

*Does that mean, Mr. Morgan, that as chief
American delegate to the peace talks, you're
saying a final agreement has been reached?*

Murray Saunders selected an old-fashioned glass,
dropped a couple of ice cubes in it and splashed a
liberal amount of Scotch over them. Conrad Morgan said with a touch of impatience:

*What I am saying, sir, is what I said. The
situation is extremely delicate, but significant
progress can be made. Is that clear? I hope it*

*is, because I would dearly appreciate the ladies
and gentlemen of the press getting it straight.*

Barking a laugh at the American delegate's dressing down of the newsman, Saunders carried his drink back to the French provincial chair in which he had been seated, and dangled one leg over an arm. He had just gotten settled when the door burst open and the man whose taped image he was watching on the screen strode into the room.

Conrad Morgan came to a momentary halt to glare at the black man, then continued across the room to slam a fat briefcase down on a spindle-legged antique table. A foot-high figurine of a seventeenth-century French woman in hoopskirt and powdered wig went flying off the table to smash on the floor. Morgan didn't even glance at it.

Flicking cigar ashes into a tray alongside his chair, Saunders said sardonically, "You're lucky those are made in the basement of the hotel."

Morgan eyed him coldly. "What the hell are you doing in my room?"

The black man took an unruffled sip of his drink and a pull on his cigar before answering. Then he said, "They told me to meet you here."

"You could have waited in the lobby." He turned to scowl at his image on the screen, still fielding reporters' questions. "Turn that goddamn thing off."

"I'm enjoying it," Saunders said, taking another sip of his Scotch.

Morgan strode past the black man to turn off the set, then stormed over to the still open door. "Come on, Harrolds!" he yelled angrily. "Get that shit in here."

"Coming, coming," a voice from the hallway called back.

Morgan stepped aside to let Edgar Harrolds enter the room. The State Department aide was about sixty, and looked older. Gray-haired and wrinkled, his once muscular body had a sagging look about it. His arms were laden with a foot-high pile of folders, papers, and documents.

"I'm not as fleet as I used to be," he remarked as he half staggered over to an antique settee and dumped his burden onto it, spilling about half the papers on the floor.

"Nor as coordinated," Morgan said acidly.

Although he was Morgan's aide, his seniority in the State Department made Edgar Harrolds far more than a mere lackey, and he was not about to take any guff from a man half his age, even though he was his superior. Just as acidly he said, "Actually, Conrad, I was always rather clumsy."

Closing the door, Morgan moved over to the closet, stripped off his coat and tie, hung them in the closet, removed his shirt, and tossed it on the closet floor. He went into the bathroom, leaving the door open, and began to run water in the sink.

"I have another engagement in twenty minutes, Saunders," he called.

Taking that as an invitation to talk to him while he washed up and redressed, Saunders climbed to his feet and ambled over to the bathroom door.

Morgan called, "Harrolds, when you get that cleaned up, make me a drink, please." This time his voice was more mellow; it was a request, not an order.

Leaning against the frame of the door, his glass in one hand and his cigar in the other, Saunders said, "So the war's over, Mr. Undersecretary."

Morgan rapidly washed and dried his face and began to shave with an electric razor. He ignored the black man's comment.

Raising his voice in order to be heard over the buzz of the razor, Saunders said with a touch of mockery, "You're practically a national treasure."

Morgan finished shaving, dropped the razor in its case, and splashed aftershave lotion on his face. He muttered to himself, but loudly enough for Saunders to hear, "Oriental son-of-a-bitch."

"Which Oriental son-of-a-bitch is that?" Saunders inquired pleasantly.

Morgan strode past him to the dresser and opened a drawer to take out a shirt. "I'd like to cut his yellow balls off," he said as he slipped into the shirt.

The black man turned to Harrolds, who was still picking up papers from the floor. "Got a pair of scissors, Harrolds?"

"When the time's right, I'll do it myself," Morgan promised grimly. Buttoning the shirt, he tucked in the tails and moved over to the closet for a fresh necktie.

Saunders said, "It sounds like your private meeting with Kuong Yin was what you guys in State call a frank discussion of the issues."

Spinning to face him, Morgan exploded, "Listen, Saunders, what is this, some kind of joke to you?"

Giving him a benign smile, Saunders said, "You could say so."

Finishing his drink, he carried the glass over to the liquor table and set it down.

"Well, it's not to me!" Morgan shouted to his back.

Lazily turning around, Saunders put his cigar in his mouth and took a puff before saying with sarcasm, "Somebody's gotta take it seriously."

Knotting his necktie without using a mirror, Morgan took a fresh jacket from the closet and put it on. In an irritated voice he said, "I told 'em I didn't need any goddamn CIA help on this thing, but they shoved you down my throat anyway."

Taking the cigar from his mouth, Saunders deliberately tapped ashes onto the rug. "They shoved me down your throat, eh?" His tone became bored. "We've done this before, Morgan. What the hell is it this time?"

Morgan went over to the dresser mirror and adjusted his necktie. With his back to Saunders, but watching him in the mirror, he asked, "How many of your CIA people are the VC holding?"

The black man frowned at Morgan's mirrored image. "I don't know what you're talking about."

"Save the bullshit for Congress," Morgan said. "How many?"

Saunders shrugged. "A hundred and fifty, maybe. Why?"

Morgan spun to face him. "They're dead," he announced bluntly.

There was a long pause, during which the black man's face became expressionless. Eventually he said, "I take it the fact we have positive information to the contrary is irrelevant."

"He wants a sacrifice," Morgan said bitterly.

Saunders examined him for some moments, then went over to stub out his cigar carefully in an ashtray. "Speak intelligibly, Morgan."

"As an addendum to the peace terms, Kuong Yin wants a sacrifice."

"Call Omaha and get him a flock of sheep," Saunders suggested.

Morgan said with forced patience, "He claims he's lost a lot of family to you people. I also think—and this isn't important, of course—but I think he's a fucking psychopath."

Saunders said with mild sarcasm, "That makes him unique in this business, doesn't it?"

Ignoring the comment, Morgan said, "In any case, we agree to write off those people as Missing in Action, they agree to call off the war and give us a lot of other people back."

Edgar Harrolds, in the act of picking up the last of the fallen papers, gave Morgan a strange, puzzled look. Saunders' face became expressionless again, but his voice took on a lethal tone.

"And you agreed?"

"I didn't agree to anything," Morgan said irritably.

Obviously disbelieving him, Saunders said angrily, "You're gonna cash in those lives for a shot at the Nobel Peace Prize, you practical son-of-a-bitch."

"Oh, don't get sanctimonious with me, Saunders," Morgan said with equal anger. "Nobody's gonna win *anything* when this war's—"

Saunders stepped on the line by snapping, "If the VC want 'em dead so bad, why don't they just kill 'em?"

Harrolds walked over to the bar and began to mix a drink. Over his shoulder he said, "They won't kill them because they're worth too much as a bargaining point."

Morgan threw his aging aide a dismissing look. "Wrong. They'll kill them as soon as they've signed the treaty. Or they'll list them MIA until they're through interrogating them or otherwise using them. So what I'm saying, Saunders, is that we at least try to get some of those people out of there."

Saunders' anger faded and something approaching respect appeared in his eyes. Edgar Harrolds carried over the light bourbon and soda he had mixed for Morgan and handed it to him. He gazed at the chief delegate searchingly, his expression less respectful than puzzled.

2

Saunders said, "I'd hate to think I've been misjudging you, Morgan."

Morgan said shortly, "That would be unfortunate. Now what do you call those commando people you have under the Phoenix umbrella?"

"The Black Tigers."

The chief delegate emitted a derisive snort. "Who the hell thinks up names like that? Black Tigers, for God's sake."

"Actually a group of us did," Harrolds told him. "Some years ago."

Saunders said, "It's a great name, Harrolds. Don't let anybody kid you."

Morgan downed half of his drink in one gulp and set the glass on the dresser. "Can they get your people out?" he asked abruptly.

Saunders shrugged. "I don't know. Very risky business. We need a couple of weeks to plan an operation."

"Forty-eight hours."

Saunders nodded agreeably. "Forty-eight hours, right. What about staging a major operation in the middle of your peace talks?"

"I'll worry about the diplomacy."

Shrugging again, the black man headed for the door. He stopped and turned with his hand on the knob when Morgan said, "Saunders."

The CIA man looked at him.

Morgan said, "I get the feeling I'm offending some sensibility in you."

Saunders merely continued to look at him.

"The American public is crying for peace," Morgan said in a statesmanlike tone. "I intend to achieve it for them."

Saunders let a slow, sardonic grin form on his face. "Like I said, you're practically a national treasure."

He pulled open the door and went on out, leaving it open. Harrolds went over to close it.

"People could at least close doors," the aging State Department aide said fussily.

Morgan picked up his glass and took another, smaller gulp. Over the top of the glass he asked, "Well, how are you holding up, Edgar?"

Harrolds hiked an eyebrow. "Fine."

With a final gulp Morgan finished the drink and set the glass back on the dresser. "You don't look fine."

"Well, I am. I'm fine."

Morgan examined him dubiously. "I don't think you like bearing the weight of all these intrigues anymore."

Harrolds moved his head in a nod of partial agreement. "The nature of evil seems to be changing. I used to believe that our work, if not moral, at least wasn't immoral."

Morgan said with mild contempt, "Sounds like you're going over the hill, Edgar."

Harrolds missed the note of contempt because he was thinking of other things. Shaking his head in sorrow, he said, "So many men being consumed and discarded like so much waste matter."

"How many Americans have died in Vietnam?" Morgan shot at him.

"Yes, yes," Harrolds said with weary resignation.

"I know the quantitative argument. Fifty thousand dead, twelve Black Tigers."

"You're talking quality, then?" Morgan asked sarcastically.

Nodding, the older man said, "Yes. The Black Tigers have always seemed the stuff of dreams and heroics to me."

"You're forgetting that we're the ones who create those illusions. When we begin to believe them as well, I'm afraid we've outlived our usefulness. No, no, Edgar. You're talking out of your asshole."

After gazing at his superior for a moment, Harrolds gave a resigned sigh. "Yes, my asshole. Talking out of my asshole." He glanced at a wristwatch. "Your appointment is in seven minutes, Conrad. We had better get moving."

When he landed at Saigon, Saunders had himself driven to a hotel that had been taken over by the United States Army to billet military police and Special Service troops. He showed an ID to the sentry guarding the front door, and was passed inside. The ID made no mention of the CIA. It identified him as a civilian advisor from the State Department to the Special Service Forces.

The four-story hotel had no elevator. Saunders climbed two flights of stairs and knocked on a door.

When a male voice called, "It's open," he opened the door and went in.

The room had twin beds against opposite walls, facing the door. Both were occupied by men sitting up with pillows to their backs, reading. On the right was a ruggedly handsome American in his early thirties, wearing nothing but undershorts, reading a book. On the left was a tall, lean Vietnamese of about the same age, fully uniformed, including combat boots, reading a Vietnamese newspaper. His uniform was identical to that of the American Army, except that it was black. He wore the insignia of a major in the South Vietnamese Army.

Closing the door behind him, Saunders said to the man in his undershorts, "Afternoon, Major."

Major John T. Booker lay down his book and swung his legs over the side of the bed to sit on its edge. "The master of Spookdom," he said amiably. "Hi 'ya, Saunders."

He had set his book down open to save his place, cover up. Glancing at the dust jacket, the black man saw that it was *Meditations* by Marcus Aurelius.

"You a Roman history buff, Major?" he asked, mildly surprised by the man's literary taste.

"History buff, but not necessarily Roman. I read old Marcus more for his moral observations than as history, though. He was one of the few completely honest politicians. Great field general, too. By most tallies he rates as one of the six greatest Roman emperors. I personally rate him number one, even above Julius Caesar."

Saunders was rather impressed, because the young major spoke with the authority of scholarship. Over the past couple of years he had developed a warm liking for Booker, but their relationship had been primarily military rather than social, and he had not been previously aware that the man was so well read.

Rising to his feet and taking a pair of black socks from the footlocker at the foot of his bed, Booker reseated himself on the bed and began to pull them on. He nodded toward the Vietnamese major, who had folded his newspaper and had also swung his feet to the floor.

"You know my bunkmate, Major Mhin Van Thieu of the ARVN, Saunders?"

"I've heard of him," the black man said. "How are you, Major?"

Rising, the man bowed formally. "Fine, sir, thank you."

Booker said, "This is Murray Saunders, Mhin, the head spook in these parts."

"Spook?" the Vietnamese said puzzledly.

"Central Intelligence Agency," Booker explained. "The mother of the Black Tigers."

Going over to the closet, Booker lifted out a freshly pressed uniform on a hanger and put it on. It was identical to Major Mhin's, except that his insignia was that of an American major. Saunders waited until he was fully dressed and was lacing his combat boots before explaining why he was there.

Then he said, "We have a mission for the Black Tigers, Major."

Booker hiked an eyebrow at him. "You don't mean a combat mission?"

"Uh-huh."

"I thought the war was over, Saunders. All my men are on pass."

"There's no cease-fire yet."

"Not officially, but there hasn't been anything but minor patrol action since the peace talks started. Nobody wants to be the war's last casualty. Tell your spook superiors to go spit up a rope."

"This wasn't ordered by the CIA," Saunders told him. "It comes straight from the Department of State."

Booker finished lacing his boots and stood up. "What's eating Foggy Bottom?"

"General Kuong Yin wants a human sacrifice as a condition of peace. There are a hundred and fifty CIA people in a special POW camp about sixty miles from Hanoi. He intends to kill them. Quietly. He doesn't want any official protest from the United States. Officially we're not to know it happened."

Booker and Mhin both stared at him. "Is he nuts?" Booker inquired.

"That opinion was expressed by a member of the State Department. In any event, the Department takes him seriously. So your mission is to go in there and get them out."

"Just like that, huh?" Booker said. "When?"

"You'll leave in forty-eight hours."

"Forty-eight hours!" Booker exploded. "We couldn't even get an intelligence report by then. You're as nuts as General Kuong."

"I'll start things moving at top priority as soon as I leave here," Saunders said. "You'll have your intelligence report, maps, everything you need. It will all be arranged. All you have to do is get your men to the airport."

"I don't like it," Booker objected. "We're practically home free, with our original dozen still more or less intact after giving the Vietcong hell for close to five years, and now you throw us this curve. We've had some Tigers shot up a bit, but we've never lost a single one of those original twelve. I'd hate to break that record, particularly after the war's over."

"It isn't over," Saunders said. "A hundred and fifty lives are at stake."

"Okay, Saunders," Booker said in a resigned voice. "We'll pull your chestnuts out of the fire." He turned to his Vietnamese roommate. "We better start rounding up the guys, Mhin. It may take us forty-eight hours to sober some of them up."

Two nights later Major John T. Booker and Major Mhin Van Thieu, in full combat gear, stood next to a jeep parked on an airstrip outside of Saigon, talking to the driver. The driver was Murray Saunders. Some yards away was a military transport plane, already loaded with the rest of the Black Tigers and ready to take off.

Booker said sourly, "Ya know, Saunders, when this war is over, you should get a job as an advance man for cancer."

Lighting one of his thin black cigars, Saunders asked, "In support of the disease or the cure?"

Mhin said, "I sometimes find it difficult to understand the American custom of joking during a time of crisis. Mr. Saunders, how sure are you of your intelligence?"

Saunders gave him a quizzical look. "I'm sure you understand, Major Mhin, that the only certain thing about intelligence is its uncertainty."

Booker said, "As usual, Saunders, you're a big help." He turned to his ARVN counterpart. "Let's go, Mhin."

Mhin, looking unhappy, started toward the waiting plane. Booker paused for a final word with Murray Saunders.

"This better be as important as your friends at State say it is."

Saunders said, "Good luck, Booker. And God bless us—everyone."

Booker regarded the black man without expression for a moment, then turned and made his way to the plane also.

3

Major Mhin was seated at the rear of the plane when Booker climbed aboard. Between him and Booker ten enlisted men were lined up on webbed seats, five on each side of the plane. Their uniforms, like those of the two majors, were jet black, and they too were in full combat gear.

In the elite Black Tigers there were no privates. The lowest rating was Corporal, or its equivalent specialist rating of Spec 4. On Booker's left, in order, were Sergeant Gordie Jones, a diminutive but scrappy man with muscles like steel springs; Sergeant 1st Class Mike Potter, tall and lean and hard-bodied; Spec 4 Mitch Henry, big and coal black; Corporal Joe Walker, lanky and awkward-looking, but with the coordination of a gold-medal athlete; and Sergeant Ron Steagle, short and stocky and with the shoulders of a linebacker. On his right were Sergeant Major Lou Goldberg, who resembled Abe Lincoln without a beard; Spec 4 Holly Washington, a powerfully built black man; Corporal Al Hakes, slightly plump but heavily muscled; Sergeant Hank Stoner, 220 pounds of granite; and Corporal Jules Finny, tall and thin and frail-looking, but as deadly as a cobra.

There was no conversation as the plane took off since the men were busily checking their weapons. But as soon as they were airborne, a general muttering arose. The tenor of it was that everyone in the army from the Pentagon on down was either crazy or retarded.

After listening to the griping with growing impatience, Booker finally shouted, "All right, you guys, knock it off."

Becoming silent, the men looked at him.

In a more moderate tone Booker said, "Now look, guys, we've been together a long time, and I know how you feel. Sure it's a rough mission, but we've had 'em before."

Sergeant Mike Potter said, "Excuse me, Major. I thought this goddamn war was supposed to be over."

"So did I," Booker told him. "But it's not. So what's your point?"

Lanky Joe Walker said, "The point is we don't wanna be the last guys killed in this friggin' war, if there's somebody else available."

Master Sergeant Lou Goldberg said, "I think they got us down for second to last."

Stocky Ron Steagle said with mock nostalgia, "Jesus, what happened to the days when Randolph Scott and John Wayne were happy to get their asses blown off for the ol' U.S. of A.?"

Big Mitch Henry turned his black face toward Steagle. "Who's Randolph Scott?"

"Come on, man," Holly Washington said. "Randolph Scott Key, the dude who wrote the national anthem."

"Oh, that Randolph Scott," Mitch said.

Booker broke into the banter to say, "All right, listen up. It's a tough operation. It's gotta be simple, quick, neat."

Mitch asked, "How simple can it be in the day-time, fercrissakes?"

"They won't be expecting it," Booker said. "We can catch them with their pants down."

Holly said, "You know, Mitch. Like the way you caught that nurse."

Booker had been standing all this time, steadying

himself by holding onto a stanchion. Now, as he started walking toward the rear of the plane, he said, "Just make sure everything works right."

Booker took a seat next to Major Mhin. The men resumed their interrupted griping.

Booker said to Mhin, "I'm afraid the men aren't too happy about this one."

"I'm not sure that I am either," the Vietnamese said. "What makes you think Hanoi will sit still for this kind of stunt?"

"I'm sure it makes some kind of sense, or they wouldn't be sending us out to do it."

"One camp," Mhin said, dissatisfied. "What good can it do? The POWs are in dozens of camps."

With a touch of impatience Booker said, "You heard Murray Saunders. The POWs in other camps aren't in danger, but they're going to execute this bunch. We're taking our best shot, Mhin. What more can we do?"

In a peevish voice Mhin said, "I do not see how a raid at this time can do anything but harm the negotiations."

Booker closed the conversation by beginning to field strip his weapon.

At the front end of the plane little Gordie Jones rubbed his mutilated left ear. "You guys can bitch it you want to," he said. "I got a score to settle, myself."

Mitch Henry said, "That's the spirit, Gordie. An ear for an ear."

Mike Potter said, "You're gonna have trouble finding an ear that size, Gordie."

Gordie growled, "I'll get me a couple of whole heads, then, and use what I need."

It was two hours before dawn when the transport plane landed with no light but that of a full moon on the dirt runway of an abandoned North

Vietnamese airstrip surrounded by jungle. The moment the plane came to a full stop, the door popped open and Booker jumped down to the ground. Major Mhin followed him out, then the enlisted men quickly jumped down. In single file they disappeared into the jungle.

They heard the plane take off again by the time they were fifty yards into the jungle. Booker led the way due west at a dogtrot for a full hour before calling a rest stop in a small clearing.

The moon was bright enough to read by. As the men spread themselves out on the ground, Booker and Mhin studied a map and oriented themselves with a compass. After a five-minute rest, Booker called the men to their feet and led the way on again, this time at merely a fast walk.

They skirted a small village shortly before dawn, and minutes later came to a large clearing that had been hacked out of the jungle. Crouched at the edge of the clearing just as first light broke, they peered out at the prisoner-of-war compound.

The compound was surrounded by an outer fence of barbed wire ten feet high, and a wooden inner fence of the same height. Inside was a cluster of POW huts and six larger buildings. The intelligence report furnished the group by Murray Saunders had described the layout of the compound, so that they knew what the larger buildings were. The largest and nearest was both the administrative headquarters of the camp and sleeping quarters for the commandant and his aides. The next largest was a stockade where recalcitrant prisoners were kept. The other four were a mess hall, an aid station, a recreation room, a storage building, and the latrine and showers.

A single guard walked sentry duty outside the barbed wire fence, and no other Vietnamese soldiers were in sight. At the moment the guard was on the far side of the compound.

After checking his watch, Booker gave the deaf sign for "eight minutes." The others checked their watches. Booker gave the sign for "do," and the various units of the team moved off to their assigned positions.

Booker, Sergeant Mike Potter, stocky Ron Steagle, and the powerfully built Holly Washington crawled on their bellies to within a few yards of the barbed-wire fence. Major Mhin and the big black Spec Four, Mitch Henry, headed for the only building outside the compound, a barracks on a rise above the camp where the guards were quartered. Plump Al Hakes, the frail-looking Jules Finny and 220-pound Hank Stoner moved part way into the clearing and waited, lying prone in the tall grass. Master Sergeant Lou Goldberg, little Gordie Jones, and the lanky Joe Walker moved on their stomachs past Booker and his three men, Goldberg finger-spelling "hi" as they went by. Almost to the wire, Goldberg signaled "stop" and "look."

The signal was for the sentry, who had turned the far right corner of the compound and was now moving toward them. At the near right corner he made a military right turn and walked past within ten feet of Goldberg and his two men, not noticing them lying there in the tall grass.

The awkward-looking Joe Walker came to his feet and moved after the guard with silent deadliness. His feet left the ground and he planted a perfectly timed thrust-kick to the man's neck from behind. The guard dropped soundlessly. Walker gripped his rifle by the barrel, hurled it off into the jungle, then dragged the body into the tall grass.

Goldberg and Gordie were crawling the rest of the way to the barbed-wire fence before the guard's body hit the ground. With wire clips they removed a half dozen three-foot strands of wire and carefully dragged them aside, leaving a gap in the fence about a yard square. Moving on to the wooden fence, they used a special spreader tool to force the slats of the fence apart until there was an A-shape gap in it two feet wide.

Booker had signaled "now" to Potter and Steagle and Holly Washington as the wires were being cut. By the time the A-shape gap in the fence had been formed, the four were right behind Goldberg and Gordie. They crawled through first. As they came to their feet, Booker, Potter, and Steagle headed for the nearest POW huts, while Holly moved toward the administrative building. Goldberg and Gordie crawled inside and took up rearguard stances.

Holly Washington, who was loaded down with grenades and explosives, stopped ten yards from the administration building and began laying out explosive devices on the ground.

Major Mhin and Mitch Henry dropped prone in the high grass fifteen yards from the guards' barracks, reached inside their uniforms, and pulled out several glistening Sirakens. Carefully they placed the death disks on the ground before them and waited.

A guard armed with a machine gun came from the barracks and headed for the compound, presumably to relieve the guard Joe Walker had taken out of action. As soon as he was past, Major Mhin rose to his feet with a Siraken in each hand. Rearing back like a big-league pitcher, the Vietnamese hurled the first metal disk through the air, transferred the second to his right hand and sent it spinning after the first.

The disks made a faint, high-pitched hum, then the first was embedded in the back of the guard's neck, and an instant later the second severed his spine. The guard dropped facedown without a sound.

Another two guards stepped from the barracks carrying rifles, and one had slammed the door behind them before either noticed the dead man and Mhin. When they did see both, and grasped that Mhin was an enemy, their rifles began to come up. Mhin scooped up two more Sirakens and sent one on its way at the same moment Mitch Henry leaped to his feet and sent one spinning. Mhin's caught one guard in the neck, Mitch's almost disappeared into the chest of the other. Aside from a slight grunt from the second man, neither made a sound as they dropped.

Mhin ran to retrieve the Sirakens from all three bodies as Mitch ran forward and began laying a demolition charge beneath the low stoop in front of the barracks. From his pack he removed two metal pins and attached electrical leads to them. Gently he pushed them into the bottom corner of the closed door, one above the other. When the door was next opened, the top pin would drop onto the bottom one, closing the circuit and discharging the explosive.

Mhin finished retrieving the Sirakens, stowed his away, and brought Mitch's two over to the black man. Mitch put them away, rose to his feet, and both men retreated twenty-five yards and crouched on their knees with their machine guns cradled in their arms, waiting for the barracks door to open.

4

Inside the compound Booker signaled Steagle "you go" and pointed to the nearest POW hut. Booker and Potter crouched on their left knees with their machine guns leveled to cover him.

Steagle went through the door of the hut fast and spun to cover all corners with his machine gun. There were a dozen sleeping pads on the dirt floor, but the place was empty. Going outside, he signaled that information to Booker and Potter.

Getting to his feet, Booker signaled "follow me" and ran toward the next nearest hut. After a quick glance inside, he shook his head and pointed to the next one. This time Steagle looked in while the other two covered him.

Turning around, Steagle said in a low voice to Booker, "How d'ya like that? We invaded the wrong country."

BLAM! Steagle's face developed a surprised expression that quickly turned to blankness. He fell with a gout of blood spurting from his chest.

Booker spun with his silenced 9-mm Uzi machine gun chattering in the direction of the shot. The North Vietnamese soldier who had fired from a corner of the aid station threw up his arms and dropped on his back.

Suddenly Vietcong troops appeared from behind and inside all six of the larger buildings and opened fire with rifles and submachine guns. The remaining five Black Tigers within the compound returned the fire with deadly accuracy, mowing down several of the enemy and driving the rest back under cover.

There were no prisoners to rescue, and they had walked into a trap, Booker realized. He signaled "go choppers," and motioned toward the gap in the wooden fence.

Over in front of the guard barracks Mhin and Mitch both tensed and looked toward the compound when they heard a rifle shot, followed by the muffled sound of Booker's silenced machine gun, then a rattle of Vietcong machine gun and rifle fire, followed by several silenced machine guns coughing. From the corner of his vision Mhin caught sight of a guard armed with a machine gun stepping around from the far side of the barracks. He spun to squeeze off a single silenced round that caught the man in the middle of the forehead.

Signaling Mitch to follow, Mhin began to run toward the POW compound. As Mitch jumped to his feet and raced after him, two other guards appeared from either side of the barracks and opened up with submachine guns. Mhin dove flat on his face in the tall grass. Mitch was hit in the back by a dozen slugs that slammed him to the ground, killing him instantly.

Al Hakes, Jules Finny, and Hank Stoner, the rearguard action team outside the compound, stationed to protect both other details, sprayed the two machine gunners.

Joe Walker, after disposing of the guard he had downed with a thrust-kick, was just crawling through the hole in the barbed wire fence when the shooting started. Seeing Booker's signal of "go choppers," he bounced to his feet and began to run toward the jungle.

Inside the compound Holly Washington had been setting explosive charges all over the camp while the other three members of his detail checked POW huts. At Major Booker's signal he dropped a final charge and raced for the gap in the wooden fence.

Mike Potter was already crawling through the gap. Lou Goldberg and little Gordie Jones sprayed machine gun fire at the buildings behind which the North Vietnamese soldiers had disappeared in order to keep them pinned down while Potter and Washington crawled through the gap in the fence.

As he fired, Gordie, anguished by the death of his buddy, Ron Steagle, whispered, "Ohhh, son-of-a-bitch!"

Up on the rise above the compound a guard in the barracks made the mistake of coming out by the front door. The entire front of the barracks exploded in a huge ball of flame that engulfed four guards running along the sides of the buildings, as well as those inside the barracks.

Joe Walker, now safely behind a thick palm at the edge of the jungle, added his fire to that of Goldberg and Gordie to cover Potter and Holly as they ran for the hole in the barbed-wire fence. When the two got through the hole, they ran for the jungle edge at an angle that took them right past the prone bodies of Mhin and Mitch Henry. There was not time to stop and check either body. Simply assuming both were dead, they ran on for cover. Diving into the thick underbrush at the edge of the clearing, they rolled behind trees.

Booker motioned for Goldberg and Gordie to crawl through the gap in the fence, but at that moment a dozen Vietcong charged from behind the administration building, firing rifles. The combined fire of Booker, Goldberg, and Gordie knocked down seven, but then all three Uzi machine guns ran out of ammunition. As the remaining five rushed at Booker with bayoneted rifles, Goldberg and Gordie each hurled Sirakens, taking out two of the five. Booker threw himself in a feet-first dive, simultaneously smashing the soles of his heavy combat boots into the Adam's apples of two. Landing on his hands and flipping himself back onto his feet, he sidestepped the bayonet thrust of the remaining VC and booted him under the chin so hard that the pop of his neck breaking was clearly audible.

Now dozens more VC poured from behind the buildings, firing rifles and submachine guns. Al Hakes, Jules Finny, and Hank Stoner, still positioned as the rearguard team outside the compound, ran forward, firing their machine guns, mowing down the Vietcong and causing the survivors to dive for cover. In the noise of battle none of them noticed the half dozen survivors of the barracks explosion who suddenly appeared on their right flank. All three of the Black Tiger rearguard went down under a barrage of machine gun fire.

Potter, Holly, and Joe Walker, who hadn't noticed the flank attackers until too late either, now blasted them from their jungle cover.

Booker, Goldberg, and Gordie hurled grenades at the buildings behind which the VC had taken cover, then Gordie tossed a grenade at the wooden fence, blasting an escape hole in it big enough for a tank. The three of them ran through it and dived for the hole in the barbed-wire fence. Booker went through first, followed by Gordie. As Lou Goldberg started through, a VC grenade exploded nearby, not near enough to wound Goldberg except superficially, but the concussion jarred him to one side, causing him to become entangled in the barbed wire.

Hearing the master sergeant scream as the barbs bit into his flesh, Booker turned to look back. A bullet caught him high in the left shoulder, knocking him down. Gordie, racing behind him, skidded to a halt and knelt over him.

Struggling to a seated position, Booker said, "Never mind me. Lou, on the wire. Get him off."

Looking back, Gordie saw Goldberg futilely floundering to get free of the barbs, but only enmeshing himself more. With bullets kicking up dirt around him, he ran back to the fence.

Potter, Holly, and Walker continued firing from their jungle concealment, driving those firing at Gordie back under cover and giving him a chance to free Goldberg.

As Gordie started to cut at the wire with his portasnips, one of the guards from the barracks who had cut down the Black Tigers' rearguard team, then in turn had been cut down by Potter, Holly, and Walker, opened slitted eyes. No more than a dozen feet from Goldberg and Gordie, he had only a superficial leg wound and had been playing dead. As Gordie snipped away, the VC rose to his feet and rushed at Gordie's back, his bayonet thrust out before him.

Goldberg, facing that way, yelled, "Gordie!"

The little man spun, skipped aside, and kicked. The kick caught the Vietnamese across both forearms, punting his rifle out of his hands to fly a dozen feet away. But the foot Gordie had on the ground slipped on the slick grass and he fell backward.

The guard flung himself on top of Gordie. The little man's feet came up and he planted them in the guard's stomach, gripped the front of his blouse with both hands, and straightened his legs. The guard did a complete somersault in the air to land on his back with the air whooshed out of him.

Instantly Gordie was on top of him, drawing his trench knife as he boarded the man. The knife flashed downward. One thrust would have been enough, but Gordie began stabbing him frenziedly, driving the long blade into his body again and again. His eyes glazed over as he forgot all about the battle, about Goldberg entangled in the barbed wire, about everything but the dead man he was hacking to pieces.

A hand grabbed his shoulder and Booker's voice said, "Gordie, he's dead, man. He's dead."

Gordie turned his head to look up, recognized Booker, but the glaze remained in his eyes. Turning back, he began hacking at the body again. Booker forcibly jerked him to his feet. Gordie stared at him; the glaze left his eyes and he sheathed his bloody knife.

Booker knelt, picked up the portasnips Gordie had dropped, and finished extricating Goldberg from the barbed wire. He pulled the master sergeant to his feet.

"Can you do it?" he asked, supporting Goldberg with his wounded arm about his waist.

Nodding, Goldberg said, "The alternative sure as shit ain't appealing."

Gordie put his arm about Goldberg's waist from the other side, and he and Booker dogtrotted him across the clearing to the cover of the jungle as the three already behind cover there kept the VC pinned down with withering fire. The three new arrivals fell flat behind trees.

"Where's Mhin?" Booker asked, glancing around.

"Dead," Holly Washington said. "Mitch too. We better stop that shoulder from bleeding, Major."

Laying down his machine gun, the black man ripped away Booker's left sleeve with one powerful tug, opened his field first-aid kit, and quickly applied a bandage. Meantime Joe Walker was examining Lou Goldberg.

"You got maybe forty punctures from that wire and grenade shrapnel," he told the Lincolnesque

Jew. "There's not that many Band-Aids among the whole crew. None of them are deep, though, and some are already clotting. You'll survive if you don't bleed to death."

"Oh, thank you, famous surgeon," Goldberg said sarcastically. "If I do bleed to death, I'll sue you for malpractice."

Looking out over the battlefield, Booker said bitterly, "Six of us. Half the team. Damn!"

With no fire coming from the jungle edge, the VC now cautiously appeared from behind buildings and began moving toward the gap in the wooden fence. Booker glanced at Holly, who held a small electronic device in his hands. At Booker's nod the black man hit the detonator switch.

A huge explosion engulfed the VC who were in the center of the compound. Then one explosion after another ripped the entire compound apart, blowing the buildings to splinters and hurling bodies into the air.

"Bye-bye, yellow brothers," Holly said.

Coming to his feet, Booker said, "All right, guys, let's hit the road."

He led the way back in the direction from which they had come. The others followed in single file.

It had taken them two hours to get from the landing strip to the POW camp, but helicopters don't require as much landing space as military transports. A large clearing in the jungle only fifteen minutes from the camp had been designated as the rendezvous point. The plan had been to ferry the Black Tigers and their rescued prisoners from there to the airstrip, where enough transport planes would be waiting to carry everyone to safety.

It took them twenty minutes instead of fifteen because of Lou Goldberg. While none of his wounds was serious, they were numerous enough to slow him down. Booker set a pace he could keep up with.

When the six neared the designated clearing, expressions of relief and anticipation formed on all six faces. Then, as they burst from the jungle into the open, all six expressions turned to consternation. There was not a helicopter in sight.

5

The men all turned to look at Booker. Joe Walker asked, "Where the hell are the choppers?"

Booker unbuckled his web belt to set his pack on the ground and drew a walkie-talkie from it. Extending the antenna, he said into it, "Nighthawk, this is Tiger One. Over."

There was no answer.

Walker said to the other enlisted men, "Somebody's gonna pay for this screwup."

"I think you're right," Lou Goldberg said. "And I think I know who."

"Yeah, us," Walker said.

"Attababy, Joe," Goldberg said, patting him on the shoulder. "Maintain that sense of humor."

"Hold it down," Booker said impatiently.

Goldberg whispered, "I don't think I could get it up now if Walker's life depended on it."

Walker whispered back, "You know, Goldberg, I don't think I like Jews."

"You're in the wrong war then, Fritz," Goldberg whispered.

Booker said into the walkie-talkie, "Come in, Nighthawk. This is Tiger One. We're at LZ and waiting pickup. Over."

There was still no answer. The enlisted men stared at the major in silence.

Retracting the antenna of the walkie-talkie, Booker put it back into his pack and shrugged the pack onto his shoulders. "Come on," he said, starting across the clearing.

"Where we going, Major?" Holly Washington asked as he fell in behind him.

"To the airstrip," Booker said. "At least the transport planes should be there."

"Solomon's navel," Goldberg groaned. "What my beat-up body needs is another two-hour hike."

Actually it was a three-hour hike, because Booker again set a pace Goldberg could manage. It was about 11:00 A.M. when they arrived at the airstrip. The sun was high, and the jungle was steaming hot.

There were no transport planes on the airstrip.

Booker set down his pack again and took out the walkie-talkie. Extending the aerial, he said into it, "Nighthawk Two, this is Tiger One. Nighthawk One failed to show at LZ, so we are waiting at MW. Over."

There was radio silence.

Booker said, "Nighthawk Two, come in, please. This is Tiger One, waiting for pickup at MW. Over."

Still nothing came from the radio.

Booker pushed home the antenna and put the walkie-talkie back into his pack. He looked at his watch, then up at the sky, searching for the transport planes. The sky was clear of everything except a single distant MIG.

Gordie said in a peculiarly high voice, "I don't get it."

Booker glanced around at the group. "I get one thing," he said grimly. "This is no ordinary screw-up."

"What kind is it, Major?" Potter asked.

"A planned one. Everything went wrong by the numbers, and that takes planning."

Lanky Joe Walker asked, "What are you saying?"

"I'm saying we've been set up."

There was unbelieving silence for some time, finally punctuated by Holly Washington breathing, "Jesus!"

"I don't get it," Gordie said plaintively. "Where are the planes?"

The men looked at him strangely. Holly said, "He just told ya, Gordie. It's a screwup."

"I like planes," Gordie said dreamily. "They're like birds." He peered at Potter. "You like birds, doncha, Mike?"

He sat down and took off his helmet. His eyes were glazed over in the same way as when he had kept hacking at the dead North Vietnamese soldier. The men stared down at him.

Goldberg said, "Oh, Christ!"

Booker said softly, "Gordie."

There was no reaction from the little man. Gently Booker put Gordie's helmet back on his head. The distant sound of a shot came from the direction they had come. Everyone listened.

After a time Mike Potter suggested uneasily, "A hunter, maybe?"

Booker said, "Or the survivors from the POW camp mistaking some poor peasant for one of us." He nodded toward Gordie. "Get him up."

The powerful Holly Washington lifted Gordie,

unresisting, to his feet, and stood with his arm about the little man's waist.

Gordie said, "I once shot a bird. My daddy took away my rifle."

Several shots sounded, this time from closer. Holly said, "Those guys are skittish. They're gonna run out of peasants before they get to us. What are we gonna do now?"

"Survive," Booker said quietly.

"Damn good idea," Lou Goldberg agreed.

Booker said crisply, "Walker, take the point. Lou, the rear."

The others looked at him in dawning and awful realization of what he meant.

In a high voice Walker said, "Jesus Christ, we're two hundred and fifty miles behind the lines. You mean we gotta walk out?"

Booker pointed into the jungle. "If you spot a taxi, flag it down."

After gazing at him for a moment, Walker shook his head and headed south into the jungle. Booker fell in behind him, and the others followed. Holly supported Gordie for a time, then tentatively took his arm from around his waist. When Gordie continued plodding along, his eyes still glazed and his face expressionless, the black man fell back to follow him.

Murray Saunders walked along the corridor of the army station hospital in Saigon until he came to Room 107. After peering through the open door, he went in and pulled the door closed behind him.

From the hospital bed John Booker regarded him without expression. Booker had the back of the bed cranked up and had been reading a book. When he closed it and set it on the nightstand, the black man saw that it was Volume V of Gibbon's

The History of the Decline and Fall of the Roman Empire.

Taking out one of his thin black cigars, the CIA agent asked, "Mind?"

Shaking his head, Booker pointed to an ash tray on the nightstand.

"Join me?" Saunders asked, extending a second cigar.

Booker shook his head again. "A taste I never developed."

"Vice, not taste," Saunders corrected. Lighting his cigar, he said around it, "Private room. The privilege of rank. Your four enlisted men are all in a ward together."

"Four?" Booker said. "You mean five."

Saunders shook his head. "Sergeant Gordie Jones is in the psycho ward."

After a moment of silence, Booker asked, "How are the others?"

"Be out in a couple of days. Just suffering from a little exhaustion. Except for Sergeant Goldberg. He has several infected wounds."

"Only several? He had about forty."

"Seems most of them healed. Tough man. You're all incredible. Two hundred and fifty miles through Vietcong infested jungle in ten days, for Christ's sake. Twenty-five miles a day through country where the peasants think they're doing good if they hack their way ten miles. You ought to go in the *Guinness Book of World Records.*"

"We had a little luck," Booker said.

"You guys make your luck." Taking the cigar from his mouth and examining the ash as an excuse not to look at the man in bed, Saunders said, "Sorry about the six you lost."

"Fortunes of war," Booker said.

Still not looking at him, Saunders said, "You don't seem sore at me."

"I don't think you're the one who shafted us. I think you got duped too."

"Thanks for the trust," the black man said, now looking at him. "It was a leak, Major. Somebody got word to the North Vietnamese that you were coming. So they moved all the prisoners and sent in a company of troops to replace them. The brass thinks maybe Major Mhin Van Thieu was a double agent."

Booker frowned. "He got killed in the operation. And took his share of Vietcong along with him. If he was a double agent, he'd have disappeared in the jungle as soon as the rest of us went in."

Saunders shrugged. "Just repeating what I was told. Obviously somebody fed the North Vietnamese the dope."

"Obviously," Booker agreed. "That explains the trap, but not the choppers and transport planes failing to show up."

"I checked that out. They claim it was just a snafu. They were scheduled to go in the following day."

"How the hell could they schedule them then?" Booker asked with exasperation. "They knew the plan was to go in fast, get the prisoners out, and double-time to the clearing where the choppers were supposed to set down."

"Just a typical fuck-up," Saunders said. "You know the army."

"They didn't go in the following day either. We would have heard them go over. We were less than twenty-five miles from the rendezvous point."

Saunders nodded. "The story I got on that is that by then they had a full intelligence report on the operation. They knew it had been a trap, and assumed you had been wiped out. They would have sent the choppers in anyway, just in case there were survivors, but their intelligence showed the rendezvous points for both the choppers and the transport planes were surrounded by Vietcong."

"So they just wrote us off," Booker said bitterly.

Saunders nodded.

"You swallowing it?" Booker asked.

"It wasn't the first botched operation of the war. They've been the rule rather than the exception."

"Not with the Black Tigers. Our operations always ran smooth. I think we were deliberately set up."

"That thought occurred to me, Major, but it doesn't make sense. I used to be a cop before the Company beckoned. In any crime investigation, it's standard procedure to look for three things: means, motive, and opportunity. In this case I can't think of any motive."

After considering this, Booker said, "We've rubbed some fur among the regular army brass for not following the book. Maybe some psycho general grabbed at a last opportunity to put us in our place."

Saunders hiked a quizzical eyebrow. "Aw, come on, Major."

"Farfetched, maybe," Booker conceded. "But generals have no corner on mental health."

"We're all a little crazy, I guess," Saunders said. He looked at the book the major had been reading. "Still pumping history, I see."

"I plan to teach it," Booker said. "Or maybe political science."

"You hold a teacher's certificate?"

Booker shook his head. "Couple of years of college is all. Gonna let Uncle Sam pay for the rest of my education."

"Where you from?" Saunders asked.

"Los Angeles."

Saunders looked pleased. "That's where my stateside office is. Maybe we could get together when we both get home."

"Sure," Booker agreed. "Give me your address."

Saunders took a card from his pocket and handed it to Booker. It contained nothing but his name, address, and telephone number. There was no indication of what his business might be.

After looking at it, Booker set it on his nightstand. "Sorry, I don't carry cards," he said. "And I can't give you an address, because I don't have any family and I was living in a college dorm when I entered the service. I'm going to have to go apartment hunting when I get back."

"You're not married, I take it."

Booker shook his head. "If I'd been married, I'd never have gotten involved in this goddamned war."

6

The graduates, in their black gowns and caps, marched across the stage one at a time as their names were called to receive their sheepskins.

"John T. Booker, Master of Arts in Political Science," the dean intoned.

Booker, his hair longer than in Vietnam, and now wearing a mustache, crossed the stage to receive both the diploma and a handclasp. He went on across it the rest of the way, down the steps, and returned to his seat at the front of the auditorium.

A half hour later, as the graduating class filed from the auditorium, waiting parents, wives of the male graduates, husbands of the female graduates, girl friends and boyfriends, embraced and congratulated the diploma bearers. No one came forward to greet Booker, however.

As he moved alone toward the parking lot, someone fell in at his side. Glancing that way, Booker saw that it was Murray Saunders. He stopped to regard the black man curiously.

"Knew you had no family or girl friend to root for you," Saunders said. "So I came as a surrogate relative." He glanced back at the cluster in front of the auditorium. "Everybody's embracing and kissing. You don't expect that, do you?"

"Only if you were prettier. Under the circumstances, I'll settle for a handshake."

The black man formally offered his hand. "Congratulations."

"Thanks."

"Understand your thesis was on the political reasons for the Vietnam War."

Booker hiked an eyebrow. "You're keeping a file on me?"

"My interest wasn't professional," Saunders said. "Just friendly. What are your plans?"

"I have a teaching fellowship at UCLA while I study for my Ph.D. Have to work for my keep."

"I meant for tonight," Saunders said. "Aren't you going to celebrate?"

"Is this an offer?"

"I'm willing to pay for dinner and a show. During dinner I'll ask you if you'd like to work for the Company. As usual you'll say no."

"Then why ask?"

Saunders grinned. "Makes it official business. I can put the evening on my expense account."

Booker shook his head. "No wonder our taxes are so high. You gonna pick me up at my place?"

"Uh-huh. About six?"

Booker nodded agreement. The two of them continued on to the parking lot.

That was in June of 1977. In September Booker began his teaching fellowship at UCLA. This involved only halftime teaching, so that the rest of his time could be devoted to attending classes himself and studying. He had gotten an apartment in West Los Angeles only a few miles from the school, and had acquired a bright yellow Porsche to take him back and forth. His income wasn't in the Porsche bracket, but he had taken the car in lieu of salary for a whole summer of test driving.

Because of his heavy work load, his social life was limited. As his evenings involved either study or correcting papers, and often both, he went out only occasionally. He was far too busy even to look for girls, let alone date with any regularity. Aside from an occasional night out with Murray Saunders, he kept his nose to the grindstone.

Even Christmas vacation was no holiday for him. He spent it doing research on his Ph.D. thesis, which he had tentatively titled: "The Psychological Causes of War in Modern Times."

Spring vacation in 1978 was going to be twelve days. Initially he had planned to study during it, too. But a few days before vacation started, he changed his mind. He was rolling along Wilshire Boulevard in his Porsche, headed for UCLA, when he saw an old man hobbling along the sidewalk, supporting himself with a cane.

I wonder how much pleasure he passed up in

struggling to "get somewhere?" Booker thought as he went by. And how much he regrets it now?

It was partly the old man, and partly that it was a beautiful, smogless spring day that made him change his mind. Suddenly he decided he wouldn't crack a book during the entire Easter vacation. He would go fishing, or boating, or maybe just spend his days lolling on the beach and his evenings cruising the singles bars in search of congenial girls.

Murray Saunders was lunching alone in the outdoor garden of a Beverly Hills restaurant when an attractive brunette with an arresting figure approached his table. She was in her late twenties, he guessed when he looked up into her smiling face. And probably single, since she wore no ring.

"Mr. Saunders?" she asked.

When he started to rise to his feet with old-fashioned courtesy, she said quickly, "Please keep your seat. I'm Marilyn Cook of the *Los Angeles Times*. May I sit down?"

"Of course," Saunders said, reseating himself. "I never run off pretty girls. I'll even buy your lunch."

As she took a seat, the girl said, "I've had lunch, thanks, but I could drink a cup of coffee."

Saunders motioned over to a waitress and ordered her a cup of coffee and a refill for himself. Having finished his sandwich, he pushed his plate aside and pulled his cup in front of him.

Taking out one of his thin cigars, he asked, "Mind?"

She shook her head. "I like the smell of cigar smoke."

"Could I offer you one?"

Smiling, she shook her head again. "It's only the smell I like. I hate the taste."

The waitress returned to pour their coffee. As

she moved off again, he lit his cigar and asked, "How'd you find me?"

"Simple. You told your answering service where you'd be."

He grinned. "And I expected you to reveal some clever reportorial dodge. What interest has the LA *Times* in me?"

"I'm doing a feature story on the famous—or maybe infamous—Black Tigers. I understand you masterminded their last mission."

Saunders' grin faded. "I wasn't in the military service, Miss Cook. I was just a civilian advisor from the State Department."

"Yes, I know that was your cover," the girl said cheerily. "Actually, of course, you were the chief CIA agent in Vietnam. Just as you now are the chief Company agent in Southern California."

Saunders looked pained. "Where did you get that information, Miss Cook?" he asked. "I'm an investment counselor."

Smiling, she said, "I won't argue the point, Mr. Saunders, because I really have no interest in your present activities. I'm only interested in that disastrous Black Tiger mission at the end of the war."

He took a puff on his cigar and a sip of his coffee. "I know something about the operation," he said cautiously. "But only from official reports. What is it you wish to know?"

"First, the makeup of the team," she said, taking a notebook and pen from her purse.

"There were only twelve in the Black Tigers. The commander was Major John T. Booker, who currently is on a teaching fellowship at UCLA, working toward his Ph.D. There was one South Vietnamese soldier, a Major Mhin Van Thieu." He thought for a moment, his forehead creased as he dredged long-ago names from his memory. "Then there was Sergeant Major Lou Goldberg, Sergeants Gordie Jones, Hank Stoner, Ron Steagle, and Mike Potter, Corporals Joe Walker, Al Hakes, and Jules Finny, and two explosives specialists named Mitch Henry and Holly Washington, both black. Mhin, Stoner, Steagle, Hakes, Finny, and Mitch Henry died during the operation."

Rapidly jotting this down in shorthand, she finished writing only an instant after he finished speaking. "You have a remarkable memory for names," she said. "Considering that all your information was derived from official reports."

He was obviously nettled at having given away his detailed knowledge of the commando group. A trifle brusquely he asked, "Anything else?"

"Yes. Just what was the mission supposed to accomplish?"

"My memory of that isn't as clear," he said. "After all, I read those reports years ago. Major Booker would be a better source of information."

She said ruefully, "Turned you off with that smart-ass crack, didn't I? I'm sorry. Shall we start over?"

"I really have only a vague memory of what went on, aside from the casualty report. But Booker was there. I'm afraid you'll have to get the rest from him."

Resignedly she closed her notebook, put it and her pen away, and rose to her feet. "Thanks for your time, Mr. Saunders. And for the lesson on how reporters should avoid editorial comment during interviews. And for the coffee."

Also rising, he said politely, "You're welcome on all three counts, Miss Cook."

He watched her as she walked away, admiring the feminine sway of her delightfully rounded bottom. As she went through the gate to the street, he tossed a bill on the table and hurried through the opposite gate leading to the restaurant parking lot.

She was just pulling out of a parking place in a green Torino when he drove off the lot. She drove to Wilshire Boulevard and turned west. A sign on the frame of her license plate read *Hertz Rentals,* he noted. It bemused him that a Los Angeles reporter would be driving a rented car.

He followed her until she turned right on Manning, which would lead her to UCLA. Satisfied that she was en route to see Booker, he drove on past, made a U-turn at the first opportunity, and returned to his office.

Except for science lab sessions and physical education, most classes at UCLA were in the mornings. But a conflict with the classes he was attending as a student required Booker to schedule his undergraduate seminar on International Relations at 1:00 P.M. It was an advanced course, restricted to juniors and seniors, and there were only seven in the class. They met around a long conference table, with Booker seated at one end.

On the last day before Easter vacation an attractive brunette with a particularly noticeable figure showed up at class. She didn't look to Booker like an undergraduate. He judged her to be about twenty-seven or twenty-eight. Because she was exceptionally attractive, he automatically looked at her left hand. She wore no wedding ring.

As she seated herself at the table, he gave her an inquiring glance.

"Margaret Cash, Professor," she said. "I'm just auditing the course."

"You're a late starter," he said. "But welcome aboard."

Instead of calling a roll, he merely glanced around

the table, noting that there were only six instead of seven students, aside from the new auditor.

"Anybody know why Charlie Abbott isn't here?" he asked as he made a note on the attendance record.

A large blonde said, "He got an early ride home for Easter vacation. Had to miss a day of classes, but he figured it was worth it. He lives in Cleveland."

Grunting, Booker took some notes from a thin leather carrying case and placed them in front of him. He said, "Today we will discuss the political events that drew us into the Vietnam War. I trust you have all read your assignments. Angelo, tell us how we first became involved."

A dark-complexioned Italian boy said, "That was under President Eisenhower. He only sent military advisors. Just a few hundred at first."

Booker nodded. "A rather innocent beginning. None of our boys were fighting, at least not officially. They were merely telling the South Vietnamese how to fight. But under subsequent administrations the United States became like a losing gambler who keeps doubling up to recoup his losses. Every time the North Vietnamese began to get the upper hand, we increased our help to the South Vietnamese, at first only with more advisors and material aid, but eventually with our own troops, no longer in a merely advisory role, but now fighting, until eventually we were doing more of the fighting than the South Vietnamese. It was a classic case of having a tiger by the tail. Those responsible for our involvement knew we never should have grabbed the tail, but they didn't know how to let go."

7

The woman who had introduced herself as Margaret Cash was impressed by John Booker's performance as an instructor. He knew his subject thoroughly, and the students obviously adored him. They hung on his words with hero-worshiping attention.

The seminar was a combination of lecture and discussion. Booker invited interruption at any point for questions by class members, and in addition periodically threw a question at one of the students. It was a stimulating and instructive session.

Booker ended the session by saying, "And so, as history slowly places it into some kind of perspective, a few things about the Vietnam War have become clear. It was a war that never should have begun, in a country we never should have entered. And its thousands of victims died without really understanding why, mainly because the reasons for the war were beyond any rules of logic or reason."

The bell rang. As the students began to rise from their seats, Booker said, "Have a nice Easter vacation, ladies and gentlemen. When you come back, we'll sing patriotic songs and pretend I didn't say any of the above."

The students filed out. Booker slipped his lecture notes back into the thin leather folder, then looked up to see the auditing student still standing there.

"I didn't get a note from the office that you were going to join the class," he said.

"That's because I lied," she said cheerily. "I never

went to the office. I just walked in off the street. I hope you don't mind my sitting in."

He regarded her quizzically. "I doubt that it classes as a felony," he said finally. "Or even as a misdemeanor."

"I'm glad you don't plan to have me arrested," she said, smiling at him. "I enjoyed your lecture. But it seems a long way from the sixties, doesn't it?"

"Yes, it does," he agreed.

"May I take you to lunch?"

"I don't eat lunch." He looked her over curiously. "Who are you?"

"I told you. Margaret Cash."

"That's only a name. *Who* are you?"

"Let me take you out to dinner and find out."

When he merely continued to examine her with curiosity, she said, "You do eat dinner?"

"I've been known to."

"I'm on an expense account," she said encouragingly.

"You're a reporter," he said, not exactly accusingly, but without enthusiasm.

"Why else would I fly all the way out here from Washington to see you?"

"I don't know. *Washington Post?*"

"What else?"

She handed him a slip of paper on which she had jotted down her name and local address during class. After glancing at it, he looked up and said, "Beverly Hilton. You must be on a generous expense account."

"I am. Pick me up at seven?"

"It's too late."

"For us?" she asked in a disappointed tone.

"For dinner. How about five-thirty?"

"At five-thirty in Washington they're still out to lunch."

"In Washington they're always out to lunch." He looked her over again, still puzzled by her. "Besides, I have a feeling this might be an interesting evening. Why not get an early start?"

With a smiling shrug she said, "You're the professor, Professor."

A block from his office on Figueroa Street in downtown Los Angeles, Murray Saunders was having his shoes shined at a street-side shoeshine stand. The bootblack was a rather plump, middle-aged Chinese. Saunders was watching girls walk by and was singing to himself in a low tone his favorite song, "Hooray for the red, white and blue, for a frog may be somebody's mother—"

His voice was a little more off than usual, because he had one of his thin cigars clamped in his teeth. The Chinese bootblack kept wincing every time Saunders hit a false note.

The bootblack gave his rag one last snap and stood back. "That's it, mister."

Saunders stopped singing, stepped down from the stand and looked down at his gleaming shoes. Taking the cigar from his mouth, he said, "Fine job, my man. Too bad you weren't born black. There could have been a future in this for you."

The bootblack neither smiled nor changed expression, but simply waited to be paid. Saunders handed him a dollar bill and started to walk away.

"Hey, mister," the Chinese called after him.

Saunders stopped and turned. The Chinese lifted a newspaper from the seat next to the one the black man had been seated in, folded it, and held it out. "You forgot your newspaper."

Saunders moved in close to accept it. The bootblack said in a very low voice, "Nineteen and twenty-four."

Saunders said loudly, "Thank you, my man."

Tucking the newspaper under his arm, Saunders strolled off down the street, his cigar again clamped between his teeth.

The building housing Saunders' office was on that section of Figueroa Street devoted to small shops, sleazy bars, and flophouses. His office was on the second floor, with the entrance to the stairs between a pawnshop and a secondhand store. It was not the sort of location to inspire the confidence of people searching for an investment counselor, which was one of the reasons Saunders had chosen it. He preferred not to be bothered by too many clients.

The door from the hall into the office had lettered on it: MURRAY SAUNDERS, INVESTMENT COUNSELING. It led into a small, unused-looking office with a desk, a typewriter, and a single file cabinet. On its far side was another door lettered: STOREROOM.

Locking the hall door behind him, Saunders crossed to the one labeled STOREROOM, unlocked it, and went in. It was a much larger office, starkly furnished, but with one unusual feature. Completely covering the far wall was a large computer with a keyboard and a read-out screen.

Locking this door behind him also, Saunders crossed to his desk and opened the newspaper the bootblack had given him to page nineteen. A small item in the lower righthand corner of the page was circled in red. It was headed: FREAK AUTO WRECK KILLS CHICAGO MAN. The item read:

```
     Chicago businessman Holly
Washington, 30, daily passed the
intersection of Damen Avenue and
35th Street twice, coming and going
to his army surplus store near the
Union Stockyards. Yesterday a
condemned building at that intersec-
```

tion was being razed when he drove by
en route to work. The iron ball of a
wrecking machine being used to knock
down the condemned building's walls
picked that moment to break loose
from its cable and smash into the
passing car. Washington was killed
instantly.

Saunders turned to page twenty-four, where
another obscure item was circled in red. This was
headed: WALL STREET BROKER STILL MISSING. The
item, datelined New York City, read:

Wall Street broker Louis Goldberg,
31, reported by his wife as kidnapped
two days ago, is still missing, and
no word has been heard from the
kidnappers. Mrs. Cylvia Goldberg told
police that two masked figures all
in black attacked her husband in broad
daylight as they got from their car in
the basement garage of their Fifth
Avenue apartment building.
Goldberg, who, as a member of the
famed commando unit of the Vietnam War,
the Black Tigers, is an expert in
unarmed combat, put up a fight,
according to Mrs. Goldberg. His
assailants were equally expert,
though, and managed to render him
unconscious with simultaneous karate
kicks. They then tied and gagged
Mrs. Goldberg, tossed her onto the
rear floor of the Goldberg Cadillac,
and escaped with the kidnap victim
in another car parked in the garage.
Mrs. Goldberg told police she
believed one of the kidnappers was a
woman, although both were dressed as
men. Police assume the motive for
the kidnapping was ransom, but no

demand for payment has yet been
received.

Folding and setting aside the newspaper, Saunders
picked up a sheet of paper in his in-box that listed
the names and army serial numbers of the six
members of the Black Tigers who had survived the
final mission. Carrying it over to the computer
keyboard, he seated himself and flipped a switch.
When the screen came to life with a greenish glow,
he punched in an access code. The word READY
appeared on the screen.

He pushed another key and the screen cleared.
Then, looking at the list of six names, he typed out:
*Washington, Holly P., Army Serial Number
37054674*. As he hit each key, the corresponding
letter or number appeared on the read-out screen,
one at a time.

No more than a second after he finished typing,
the following information began appearing on the
screen just below what he had typed, one row at a
time:

4–25–48
E–4, Explosives Expert—Vietnam
Black Tiger Team
Hon Discharge 2–25–74
See file 2727ML8

A frown appeared on Saunders' face as he pushed
the key clearing the screen. Then he typed in
2727ML8, and, one by one, those figures appeared
on the screen. Moments after he finished, this read-
out appeared:

Washington, Holly P. 37054674
Operation Sandstone 3–75

Yemen
DA Conf 631RQ4
Sanc Auth 1 1 1 1 1 1 1 1 1 1
Comp

Saunders gazed at the read-out as though he couldn't believe his eyes. Automatically lighting another cigar, he leaned back in his chair and stared at the screen for a long time. Finally he leaned forward, cleared the screen, and typed a new message. This time it read: *Goldberg, Louis T., Army Serial Number 56263125*. The read-out below this read:

9–18–47
Sgt Maj—Vietnam
Black Tiger Team
Hon Discharge 2–25–74
See file 2727ML9

Again frowning, Saunders cleared the screen and typed in 2727ML9. Moments later, this read-out appeared:

Goldberg, Louis J. 56263125
Operation Sandstone 3–75
Yemen
DA Conf 631RQ4
Sanc Auth 1 1 1 1 1 1 1 1 1 1
Comp

This time Saunders' expression was not one of disbelief, but merely of cynicism. Clearing the screen again, he began typing: *Booker, John T., Army Serial Number 0–454279*.

8

Booker arrived at the Beverly Hilton at exactly 5:30 P.M. to find Margaret waiting in the lobby. That day she had worn a plain beige suit. Now she had on a clinging rose-colored dress that accented every line of her remarkable body. By the way she jiggled when she rose to her feet, Booker realized she was wearing no brassiere.

"I'm parked out back," he said, steering her toward the exit to the parking lot.

When he held the door of the Porsche open for her, she regarded it with surprise. "Quite a car," she said. "But not exactly ideal for going stoplight to stoplight."

"Not unless they're a couple of hundred miles apart," Booker agreed.

She slid in and he rounded the car to climb behind the wheel.

Still referring to the car, she said, "Pretty much for a graduate student."

"Did some test driving," Booker told her. "Like a damned fool took the car instead of a salary. You have a preference for any particular type of food?"

"Not really," she said. "I'm omnivorous. I run the gamut from Albanian shish kebab to Zanzibar snails."

"What are Zanzibar snails?" he asked.

"I don't know," she said, grinning. "I just made them up."

He pulled off the lot and turned east on Wilshire Boulevard. "Like Italian?"

"Love it. And Greek and Chinese and American, or what have you. I told you I'm omnivorous. Only two things I can't eat."

"What are those?"

"Brains and fish-eye soup. Probably I'd even like those if I ever got up the courage to taste them, but to date I've always chickened out."

"I like an easy-to-please woman who knows where to draw the line," he said. "It's Italian."

He continued along Wilshire, through Beverly Hills, toward downtown Los Angeles. At Highland Avenue in Hollywood they were stopped by a red light. Slowing up behind them was the cab section of a cross-country truck, without the trailer attached to it.

It didn't slow quite enough. There was a gentle bump as its front bumper barely nudged the rear bumper of the Porsche. Booker glanced around with a frown, but said nothing, as the nudge had been too slight to cause any damage. As he faced forward again, the truck's engine roared and powerful pressure was exerted on the sports car's rear bumper, forcing it forward. Booker jammed on the brakes to keep from being shoved out into the heavy cross traffic.

"What the hell is that guy trying to do?" he said angrily.

The roar of the truck engine grew even louder, and the pressure became such that the brakes could no longer hold the Porsche back. At that moment there was a momentary gap in the cross traffic, not wide enough to cross safely, but Booker didn't have the choice of waiting for a wider gap.

"Hang on," he said to Margaret as his foot left the brake and slammed down on the accelerator.

With screaming tires the yellow sports car darted through the narrow gap in the cross traffic. A half dozen sets of brakes screeched, and one of the cars the Porsche cut in front of was rearended by the car behind it. When nearly across the intersection, Booker spun the wheel and hit the brakes. The powerful sports car did an about-face of 180 degrees, coming to rest by the curb on the other side of the street, facing back toward the truck.

Booker was out of the car the instant it came to a full halt. Cross traffic had come to a snarled halt also, and the man who had been rearended was getting out of his car to stalk menacingly back to the one that had rearended him. Booker raced across the street, jumped on the running board of the truck cab, pulled open the door, and got two handfuls of the driver's shirt front. The truck driver was rather sizeable, but Booker jerked him across the seat as though he were a rag doll.

"All right, you son-of-a-bitch," Booker said. "What's going on?"

The truck driver said in a plaintive voice, "Hey, man, take it easy. The goddamn gas pedal is stuck."

Booker became aware that the truck engine was still racing, although the truck was no longer in gear. Looking down at the floorboard, he saw that the man's foot was not on the accelerator.

Releasing his double grip, Booker said, "Why the hell didn't you take it out of gear when you saw it was pushing me out into traffic?"

"It's out of gear."

"Now, yeah. Your reactions are too slow for a truck driver, buddy. You better get a different job. Why the hell don't you stop that thing from roaring by killing the engine?"

"I thought maybe I could kick the pedal free."

The driver banged his foot on the stuck pedal a

couple of times. The engine continued to race. He gave it one more kick, and suddenly it was idling.

The light turned green at that moment. Shifting into gear, the truck driver gunned the cab forward, at the same time reaching out to push Booker in the chest. Booker half fell and half jumped from the running board to land on his feet unhurt. The semitractor screeched around the corner in a right turn and raced south on Highland.

Having the green light with him, Booker ran back across the street and jumped into the Porsche. There was no way to follow the semitractor, though, because the intersection was still blocked on that side of the street by the two cars involved in the minor accident. The drivers of both were now out in the middle of the street, having a shoving match.

Stalled traffic alongside of him had Booker blocked in. He backed up onto the sidewalk, backed along it to a driveway, backed into the driveway, pulled forward and made a left turn. Rounding the block, he came out on Highland a block south of Wilshire and gunned the Porsche south for a few blocks. When he failed to spot the truck cab, he gave up and pulled over to the curb.

Margaret, who had been hanging onto the door handle ever since Booker started to back along the sidewalk, said in a shaken voice, "That was quite an experience."

"Yeah," Booker said. "Still hungry?"

"I might be in another hour, when my stomach stops quivering."

"How about a drink at my place, then?" he suggested.

"I could use one."

Booker's place in West Los Angeles was what southern Californians call a "bachelor apartment." That didn't mean it was a type restricted to men, but only that it wasn't big enough for more than one tenant. It consisted of a single large room with a dining area at one end and living room furniture at the other. The living room area converted to a bedroom when the sofa bed was pulled out.

Opposite the front door was a kitchen alcove with doors off either side of it. One led into a large closet, the other into a bathroom. The place was plainly and masculinely furnished with a redwood picnic table in the dining area and with brown leather-covered furniture in the living area. The walls were lined with bookshelves.

Looking around, Margaret said, "It's nice, but if I lived here, I'd add some pink and some lace doilies."

"There isn't room for you to live here," Booker told her. "But thanks for the offer."

"Smart-ass," she said, making a face at his back as he went into the kitchen alcove to mix drinks.

"Manhattan or martini?" he asked.

"I'm omniliquorous too, if there is such a word. Whatever you're having."

He mixed two martinis and carried them over to the table. She sat and he seated himself across from her. Both raised their glasses.

"To less excitement," he said.

"I'll drink to that," she told him. "Is every day of your life as exciting as this?"

"Not quite." He examined her so thoroughly that she blushed. "But I have a feeling that things are about to change. You've got something to say, say it."

"My, you're blunt."

"It's been mentioned to me," he admitted.

She took a sip of her drink before speaking, studying him over the top of her glass. Finally she said, "You were on a top secret mission to rescue some POWs at the end of the war."

Taking a sip of his drink also, Booker said nothing.

"No response?" she said.

"I get it," he said, pretending sudden enlightenment. "You're writing a book about the war."

"Something like that. When you arrived at the camp, there were no POWs. Only VC. You lost most of your men."

"Not most. Exactly half. I wonder who told you about that? It was all top secret."

His tone was one of amused indulgence. Flushing slightly, she asked, "Shall I go on?"

He reached across to pick up her left hand and look at it. "Are you married?"

She didn't withdraw her hand, but she refused to be sidetracked. Doggedly she continued, "After the raid, you were to be met and flown by helicopter to where some military transport planes were waiting. Neither the helicopters nor the transport planes ever showed up. So you marched out of the jungle with five of your men."

Finishing his drink and setting down the glass, Booker asked good-naturedly, "Do you fool around?"

"It should have taken you twenty-five days to get out of the jungle, according to expert opinion. Instead, you made it in ten. Then you were, as they say, debriefed for two months in a hospital."

Getting up, Booker went into the kitchen alcove, opened the refrigerator, and peered in.

Margaret said, "Officially you were suffering from exposure, exhaustion, and a bullet wound. One of your men also had a number of minor wounds, and one ended up in the psycho ward, but you got the rest out relatively unscathed. Nothing was ever printed about that strange sortie. Why not?"

Booker held up an egg. "How about something to eat?"

"What happened to those POWs who weren't there to be rescued? Have they been returned? Are they MIA? Are they dead? Will anybody admit that they existed? Will you speak to any of those questions? Your choice."

"Now, what can you do with one egg?" Booker asked, gazing at it.

Giving up, Margaret got to her feet, tossed off the rest of her drink and carried both glasses over to the sink. Then she took the egg from his hand and pushed him aside.

"Watch out," she said. Opening the refrigerator, she peered inside. There was some parsley, one clove of garlic, and a stack of college examination books. "Nice selection."

"I try to keep a full larder," Booker said modestly.

Pointing to the examination books, she said, "I suppose we could sauté these."

"I've already burned midnight oil over them," he said. "And I hate leftovers."

Closing the refrigerator, she opened the freezer compartment. After peering in, she asked, "How about sharing a piece of frozen halibut?"

"Yukkk!" he said. "I'm not as omnivorous as you."

She closed the freezer compartment.

¶

Glancing around, Margaret spotted a small combination folding stepladder and stool. She placed it in front of the work counter and climbed up on it to open the cupboard doors. Booker examined her legs with interest.

"Your unit was part of Operation Phoenix," she said with her back to him. "Its job was to—'neutralize,' I believe they called it—Vietcong undercover agents. You were also assigned to rescue our own POWs."

In an admiring voice he said, "You're very intense for a girl with such great legs."

Gazing into the cupboard, she asked, "How about one egg with sauerkraut and smoked oysters?"

Handing him the cans from the cupboard, she jumped down from the stepladder-stool. He set the cans on the work counter, folded up the little ladder, and leaned it against the wall where it had been.

Margaret opened the sauerkraut, heated it in a pan and scrambled the egg. Meantime Booker found some crackers, set the table, opened the oysters and a bottle of wine, and put candles on the table.

"Will you tell me anything?" Margaret asked.

Emitting a resigned sigh, Booker said, "If I want to eat in peace, I suppose I have to. Has anyone ever told you you're obnoxiously persistent?"

Nodding, she said, "My mother and father said it repeatedly. But it's what makes me such a good interviewer."

Carrying the frying pan over to the table, she divided the scrambled egg with a spatula and put a portion on each plate. While she was returning to the stove for the pan of sauerkraut, Booker lit the candles and poured the wine. He seated himself on the side of the table away from the kitchen alcove, and after serving the sauerkraut, she sat across from him.

"All right, tell me," she said.

"There's really not much to tell. Walking out of that jungle, I was out of my head with fury. In the hospital, they said that VC intelligence had cracked our security. Reasonable possibility. They said the failure of the choppers and planes to show up was just an administrative goof-up. They'd been scheduled for the next day. Reasonable possibility there. Then they said that by the next day, their intelligence told them about the trap we'd run into, and that both the landing areas for the choppers and the transports were surrounded by VC. They assumed we were all dead anyway, so they just wrote us off."

"Did you believe it?"

"Sure I believed it. I wanted to believe it. In the hospital I told myself, the war's over. You lived through it. Now put it behind you. I could spend years trying to find out if somebody set us up. And if I found him, it would most likely be someone I couldn't get to anyway. You heat sauerkraut very well."

"I took domestic science in high school. You open smoked oyster cans very well. What if it were someone you could get to?"

Booker cleared his palate with a sip of wine. "I decided not to waste my life to avenge something I'd survived. It's over. And I want to keep it that way."

Setting down her fork, Margaret sipped wine too. "I don't believe you really feel that way."

He shrugged. For a few moments they ate in silence. Then he said, "Why are you asking these questions?"

"I can't tell you."

"Then stop asking them," he said grumpily.

"Don't be a grouch. I think you've come to despise your involvement in that war. Why don't you talk to me about what you know?"

"I'd rather talk about you."

Again they ate in silence for a time. It didn't take long to finish both plates. Margaret carried the empty plates over to the sink and put on the kettle for instant coffee. Getting down two cups, she spooned coffee into them, then returned to the table.

"I met a man at a cocktail party in Washington," she said. "He was what the newspapers call a 'high-ranking government official.' . . . He was also very, very drunk. We talked for a long time. The Scotch seemed to break some barrier in his mind. I'm not sure why, but he told me some things that I probably shouldn't have heard."

"Maybe it's because you're such a good listener."

"He mentioned the Black Tigers."

"How's the coffee coming?"

"Don't try to change the subject. The kettle will whistle when it's ready to pour."

"No, it won't. The whistle gadget is broken."

She glanced over her shoulder, then faced him again. "Well, we can see the steam." She looked him up and down. "John T. Booker, a man taking a Ph.D. in political science who used to be a member of the CIA. Sounds schizophrenic."

"I was never a member of the CIA," Booker protested.

"The Black Tigers was organized by the CIA."

Booker gazed at her. "I didn't know the Freedom

of Information Act was that effective," he said eventually.

"It's not, but I am. Why did you join the Special Forces?"

"I was drafted," he lied.

"You enlisted and then volunteered for Special Forces. What do you think about Conrad Morgan being named Secretary of State Designate?"

He looked startled by the abrupt change of direction. "Nothing," he said in a tone implying the question of what that had to do with the conversation.

"Not interested, huh?"

"I'm only interested in finding out what you're not telling me."

Smiling, she said, "Who's going to tell who first what he or she isn't telling?"

He smiled back. "Steam's coming out of the kettle."

Rising, she went over to pour boiling water into the two cups, stir them, and bring them over to the table.

Reseating herself, she said, "Maybe I'll tell you before the evening is over. Or in the morning. How about the morning?" After a pause, she added, "But I forgot. The place isn't big enough for two."

"Only on a permanent basis," he said. "There's plenty of guest room. The sofa makes up into a double bed."

"I do admire a hospitable man," she said. "But is it hospitality, or just horniness?"

After considering, he admitted. "Well, I doubt that I would have made the offer if you were a fellow."

When they finished their coffee, Margaret started to do the dishes. Booker went over to pull out the sofa and make it into a double bed. Margaret glanced over at him, then at the clock over the stove.

"It's only seven-fifteen," she said. "You can't go to bed that early."

"I wasn't planning on sleep just yet."

After a moment of thinking this over, she said, "Oh. Mind if I finish the dishes first?"

"Yes."

"All right," she said submissively, turning off the hot water she was running in the sink and just letting the dishes soak.

He was setting an alarm clock when she came over to the bed and began to undress.

"You don't have school tomorrow," she said. "It's Easter vacation, remember?"

"I get up early to jog," he said. "I'll try not to disturb you."

"An alarm clock going off in my ear won't disturb me?" Then she shrugged. "The wages of sin, I suppose."

Although they spent the next eleven hours in bed, they got only intermittent sleep. Neither was a very sound sleeper, and every time one woke up, the other did also, and they reached for each other. Between lovemaking and simple insomnia, they slept only about half the time they were in bed.

Just as it started to get light, Booker had a nightmare. His mutterings awakened her, and she sat up to look down at him. His face was beaded with sweat and his teeth were clenched together.

"Ron, Al, Hank, Jules," he whispered in an agonized voice. "God, they got Mitch too." Suddenly he sat straight up. "Bastards!" he yelled. "Murdering bastards!"

He popped awake to find Margaret staring at him. He gazed at her sheepishly.

"Bad dream?" she asked.

"Yeah."

"What?"

"Nothing," he said dismissingly.

Both had been sleeping nude. She laid a soothing hand on his bare shoulder. He gave the hand a little love pat, then jumped from bed. Padding to the bathroom and leaving the door open, he switched on the light, ran cold water in the sink, and slapped some on his face.

Margaret came over to stand in the bathroom doorway. "You don't sleep well," she said.

He glanced at her. "No?"

"How I know is I don't either. You're very good at what we did before we went to bed to sleep, though."

He smiled at her. "So are you."

She curtsied, holding out the skirt of an invisible dress. The alarm clock went off, startling her. She ran over to shut it off. There was no button on the back to press in, and she couldn't figure out how to turn it off.

"How the hell do you shut this off?" she called.

"You push in the thingamajig," he called back.

"There isn't any thingamajig."

Giving up, she set the clock down and simply let it wind down. The clanging gradually became less strident, and finally stopped.

Booker had closed the bathroom door. She yelled through it, "Why does someone who doesn't sleep well need an alarm with the timbre of Big Ben that can't be turned off?"

There was no answer. When Booker emerged from the bathroom, he began to slip into his jogging suit.

"Where are you going?" she asked.

"To run."

"I jog myself."

"Come along," he invited.

"I had sufficient exercise last night," she said. "Breakfast?"

He shrugged. "If you can find anything."

"Ah, of course. You don't eat breakfast."

Taking her into his arms, he kissed her soundly. She tightened her arms about his neck and began to breathe a little heavily.

Breaking away, he said, "It's a chore to put this outfit on. I don't want to have to take it off, then put it on again."

"I knew it would happen," she said in mock despair. "The honeymoon is over."

"Only suspended," he told her. "I'll see you in exactly twenty-seven minutes, and when I get back, we can talk about"—he allowed a suggestive leer to creep into his voice—"breakfast."

"Shall I put on my clothes?" she asked.

"I didn't plan on a formal breakfast."

Smiling, she said, "I'll have it ready in twenty-seven minutes."

He went out and closed the door behind him.

10

Knowing John Booker's habits, Murray Saunders parked a quarter of the way down the street from Booker's apartment at twenty minutes to seven. At exactly a quarter to seven Booker came out in his jogging clothes and started to run along the street.

Saunders started the car, pulled up next to him, and kept pace with his jogging.

Glancing that way and recognizing Saunders, Booker said, "I gave at the office."

"Pull over, John," Saunders said. "Gasoline is expensive."

Saunders pulled ahead slightly, then nosed in to the curb. Booker came to a halt and waited for the black man to get out.

"Why don't you get an honest job?" Booker asked as Saunders came over to him.

"What? And give up my cloak and dagger?"

Saunders reached into his breast pocket, took out a long, thin cigar, and lighted it. "John, we have to talk," he said.

"I thought we were." Booker sniffed the aroma of the cigar. "I know better than to ask where you've been, but that cigar smells like pure Havana."

"Fringe benefits, John. What did you talk to Marilyn Cook about?"

"Do I know her?"

"Come on, John. The reporter from the *Los Angeles Times* who seems to have more answers than questions."

Booker looked puzzled. "You wouldn't be talking about a reporter from the *Washington Post* named Margaret Cash, would you?"

Saunders eyed him curiously. "Brunette, twenty-sevenish, good-looking, eye-bugging figure?"

"You're talking about her."

"She told me Marilyn Cook. Next guy'll get Myrna Catt or Marilee Case. She's obviously into the Ms and Cs. Also obviously, I goofed."

"How's that?" Booker asked.

"Usually I check out anybody who's checking me out. I even thought it funny that a local reporter was driving a rented car. But I didn't even phone the *Times* to find out if they had a reporter named Marilyn Cook. Probably old age."

"More likely her innocent air. I told her about a long walk I took a few years ago. What did you tell her about?"

"Not much. The names of the Black Tigers. Then something made me pull in my horns. Somebody told her more about that mission than you and I know."

"That scar's ugly," Booker said. "But it's healed."

Saunders blew a perfect smoke ring and watched it disintegrate. "I think it's about to be reopened."

"By her? No way."

"The lady, as we say in the trade, is just the tip of the iceberg."

With mock admiration Booker said, "You guys sure have a way with words."

"Then listen to these," Saunders suggested. "You're back in it, John, whether you want to be or not."

Booker stared at him. "Back in what?"

"The Black Tigers."

"They were disbanded, for Christ's sake."

"Wanna come over to my office and look at a new gadget I've got?"

"I told a house guest I'd be back in twenty-seven minutes. What kind of gadget?"

"A computer hooked into every government file there is. Would you like to see the high school grades of the Speaker of the House?"

"It doesn't sound as interesting as breakfast with my house guest."

Saunders went over and held open the curbside door of the car. "Get in, John. All kidding aside, this is important. If I may coin a phrase, it's a matter of life and death."

"You guys really do have a way with words," Booker said. He got in the car.

While he had seen Saunders' apartment on a number of occasions, Booker had never before been to his office. He looked bemused at the sign on the outer door proclaiming it to be the office of an investment counselor. He looked even more bemused when Saunders unlocked the door labeled STOREROOM and led the way into the inner office.

"Just like *The Man From Uncle*," Booker said as the CIA agent locked them in. "Is all this really necessary?"

"The Company boss says so. Ours not to question why, ours but—"

"I read it in high school," Booker interrupted. He looked at the blank computer screen. "Tell me about your new toy."

"Wanna play pong with an agent in Afghanistan?"

"Some other time."

Saunders walked over to the machine and turned it on. Seating himself before the keyboard, he said, "Okay, we'll play a different game, but I don't think you're gonna like it as well."

The screen was now glowing a light green. Saunders punched an access code and the word READY appeared.

Pushing a key to clear the screen, he checked his list of six names and typed out: *Booker, John T., Army Serial Number 0–454279.*

Immediately after that appeared on the screen, there appeared below it one line at a time:

3–31–41
Major—Vietnam
Black Tiger Team Commandant

Hon Discharge 2–25–74
See File 1389PQ4

Booker said, "I think I'd rather play pong with that guy in Afghanistan."

Ignoring the comment, Saunders said, "See that file number? When I punch in that number, it's supposed to tell me your current address and occupation."

The file number appeared on the screen as Saunders typed it, then, one line at a time, other information appeared below it:

1389PQ4
Booker, John T. 0–454279
Operation Sandstone 3–75
Yemen
DA Conf 631RQ4
Sanc Auth 1 1 1 1 1 1 1 1 1 1

"Operation Sandstone, huh?" Booker said. "I don't seem to recall that one."

"There was no Operation Sandstone. See the line with 'DA' on it?"

Booker nodded.

"That means that sometime during an operation that never happened, it was confirmed that you were a double agent."

Booker stared from the screen to Saunders.

Saunders said, "You see that 'Sanc Auth', then the series of 1s?"

Gazing at the screen, Booker said slowly, "I've heard how the Company handles double agents. There's a contract out on me."

"Correct."

"Why?"

"I suspect that reporter found out something she shouldn't have. What did she tell you?"

"She said somebody talked to her about the mission. A high government official who got drunk at a cocktail party in Washington. I didn't want to hear about it."

"That's why ostriches die young. Whoever talked to her apparently has decided to rectify his error."

Still staring at the screen, Booker asked, "Well, who the hell can get into this machine and put out a hit on me?"

"The President, the Secretaries, and a few Undersecretaries of Defense and State, the directors of the FBI and the CIA, the chairman of the National Security Council, and the chairman of the Joint Chiefs of Staff."

"Thank God it's nobody important," Booker said sardonically. "Jesus, Murray, this is crazy."

"It's not just you," Saunders said. "A funny rumor seeped to me a while back that something was brewing about the Black Tigers. That gave me a reason to check out all five of the other guys who came out of the jungle with you. There's contracts on all of you."

"Jesus!"

"I learned about it a little late. Not until yesterday afternoon, as a matter of fact. I tried to phone you about five-thirty, but there was no answer."

"I was out. What do you mean, you were a little late?"

"Holly Washington is dead, and I think Lou Goldberg is too."

This news hit Booker hard. "Oh, Jesus," he said. Then he gave Saunders a searching look. "Was it your people?"

"I don't know."

"Find out," Booker said bluntly.

Saunders spread his hands in a gesture of helplessness. "Look, first I get a tip that something's brewing, too late to save Holly and Lou. Then I meet a girl who knows more about that goddamn raid than anyone should. Then there's the fact that I'm the guy who sent you on it."

"So?"

"I'm not on the computer—yet. But it's a damn good bet that if I try to dig up any information that isn't already in the memory bank, my name will appear on the hit parade along with the rest of you."

"Can't you at least warn the rest of 'em? Protect 'em?"

Switching off the machine, Saunders rose from his seat and went over to his desk. From a top drawer he took out a strip of computer read-out tape with a list of names and addresses on it.

"You can," he said. "Last known addresses."

Scanning the printout, Booker started to say, "Damn it, Murray, I can't just—" then came to an abrupt halt to stare at the tape. "Mhin Van Thieu? What the hell is Mhin's name doing on here? Mhin was killed in the raid."

"Evidently not," Saunders said. "First listed MIA, then POW. Released at the end of the war. We apparently paid him off by bringing him into this country. Cooking for some Pekin-style restaurant in San Francisco. Specializes in fried dumplings."

"That's great," Booker said sarcastically. "What else do you know that you may have forgotten to tell me?"

"Funny you should ask that," Saunders said, furrowing his brow. "There is something else I've been trying to remember, and should remember, but for the life of me, I can't dredge it up."

"More likely, for the life of me," Booker said bitterly. "That helps a lot."

Saunders said with a mixture of regret and sympathy, "John, there's a lot I can't help you with. The Company has too many eyes. You're gonna have to warn those guys yourself."

"This is my life you're screwing with, Murray."

"It's mine, too, friend. You want a ride home?"

Booker stared at him. "Well, I sure as hell didn't plan to jog from Figueroa Street to West Los Angeles."

11

When Booker got back to his apartment, he found Margaret gone, the dishes washed and put away, and the bed made back into a sofa. A note in lipstick on the bathroom mirror read:

Waited 28 minutes. Halibut in oven. Left you half. Pretend it's dinner. XOXOXO, M.

He went back into the kitchen and looked into the oven. The halibut was wrapped in a piece of foil and the oven had been left on 250.

Making some instant coffee, he turned off the oven and had the fish for breakfast standing up at the work counter. There was no bread in the house, so he had a couple of crackers with it.

Afterward he showered, then had to clean the mirror before he could shave. When he was dressed, he lay on the sofa, stared at the ceiling, and thought.

His thoughts flashed back to the night in 1973 when he and Mhin stood talking to Murray Saunders at an airstrip outside of Saigon. He had said, "You know, Saunders, when this war is over, you should get a job as an advance man for cancer."

He had liked the black man at that time, but they hadn't really known each other well enough even to be on a first-name basis. Only since the war had they become close friends. Saunders had just demonstrated how close he considered the friendship by warning Booker of what he was up against. The CIA was a close-knit fraternity that demanded loyalty to what its members called the Company above all other loyalties. Under its philosophy, it would be unforgivable even to warn your mother that she was on the Sanction Authorized list. Saunders had both violated his code and risked his life to tip off Booker.

A contract was out on him. The thought that an agency of the United States Government could order seven men murdered as casually as the Mafia ordered hits was monstrous. The moral justification, of course, was that he and the others were traitors, and thus deserved death. But even if the charges had been true, the process violated every constitutional standard of justice. In America you were supposed to have the constitutional right to face your accuser and make him prove his charges beyond all reasonable doubt. And sentences were supposed to be handed down only by courts of law. But Booker and the other Black Tigers had been tried, found guilty, and condemned by some face-less bureaucrat, on falsified evidence.

Nor was there any appeal. No one would be-lieve Booker's claim that the CIA meant to kill him. Spokesmen for the Agency would simply deny it. Publicly charging that he had been fingered might delay the inevitable, but eventually, when whatever furor Booker managed to raise had died down, a quiet accident would happen. There would be no way to escape it, because it was absolutely impossible to remain alert twenty-four hours a day, three hundred and sixty-five days a year.

Another, more recent memory drifted into Booker's mind. The truck cab, with its engine roar-ing, was trying to shove the Porsche into the murderous cross traffic of Highland Avenue. That had been no accident, he suddenly realized. That had been part of *Sanc Auth 1111111111*.

Now his thoughts darted back to that fateful time in Vietnam again. Joe Walker, indignant over the failure of the helicopters to be at the assigned spot, had said, "Somebody's gonna pay for this screwup." Later, at the airstrip where the trans-port planes failed to show also, Holly Washington had asked, "What are we gonna do now?" and Booker had replied, "Survive."

"Survive!" he thought. It was still the basic rule of life. "Survive!"

"That's why ostriches die young," Murray Saunders had said. It was true. If Booker simply sat and waited with his head in the sand, he probably would be dead within days.

Some general had said, "The best defense is at-tack." In this case it seemed to Booker the only de-fense. "Survive!" he thought again. "Attack!"

Abruptly sitting up, he reached over to the end

table where he had set the computer printout given him by Saunders, picked it up, and looked at it.

"All right, Saunders, you son-of-a-bitch," he said in a tone of rough affection. "We'll do it your way."

One of the seven names on the list was Booker's. Saunders had drawn lines through the names of Holly Washington and Lou Goldberg, leaving only four aside from Booker. Joe Walker's address was Guaymas, Mexico. Mike Potter's was Squaw Valley. Gordie Jones lived in San Diego, and Mhin Van Thieu was listed as contactable at the Happy Pekin Inn in San Francisco, presumably the restaurant where he worked as a cook.

Booker picked up the phone and dialed the operator. "Can you get me Information in Guaymas, Mexico?" he asked.

"What state is that, sir?"

"Sonora."

"The name of the person you wish to phone?"

"Joseph Walker, Four-ninety-five Camino del Playa. In English that's Beach Road."

"Just a moment, please. I'll see if I can get you the number."

It was closer to five minutes. The operator periodically came back on the line to report that she was still trying. Eventually she said, "I'm sorry, sir, but they have no phone listed either under that name or at that address. The Mexican operator says that's an area of fishing shacks that are generally without utilities."

"Okay," Booker said. "Thanks anyway. Now can you get me Squaw Valley Information?"

"You can dial that direct, sir. Just dial One, the area code, then Five-five-five, One-two-one-two."

"Okay, what's the Squaw Valley area code?"

When the operator gave him that, he marked it down behind Mike Potter's name, then said, "While

I have you on the phone, you may as well give me San Diego's and San Francisco's area codes, too."

When he had listed the other two numbers behind Gordie Jones' and Mhin's names, he dialed Squaw Valley Information and got Mike Potter's number. But when he dialed it, he got no answer.

He called San Francisco Information and got the number of the Happy Pekin Inn. When he dialed that, a man with a strong Chinese accent answered the phone.

"Him glo away," he said when Booker asked for Mhin. "Him no belong this place now."

"Where did he go?" Booker asked.

"Him no say. Glotta glo now. Somebody want slervice chop-chop. Bly-bly."

Booker found himself holding a dead phone. He dialed San Diego Information and got Gordie Jones' number. When he dialed it, a woman answered.

"Hello?" she said.

"Gordie Jones, please."

"He's not here."

"Is this his wife?" Booker asked.

"Yes," she said, in a tone suggesting she was a little reluctant to admit it.

"I'm John Booker. He's probably mentioned me."

"Not to me, mister."

"Oh. Well, can you tell me how to get in touch with him?"

"You can't. He's on the train."

"Where is he going?" Booker asked.

"Not that kind of train. This one don't go no-where. His uncle's. Sheffield's Train-o-rama at Traveltown. It's kind of an amusement park."

"I see," Booker said. "Can I call him there?"

"Nope. He ain't got no phone there. We don't owe you money, do we, mister?"

"No, I'm just an old friend. It's rather important that I get in touch with your husband."

"Well, call tonight," she said. "He gets home about six-thirty."

Hanging up, Booker thought ruefully that the miracle of modern communication wasn't as miraculous as it was touted to be. He had managed to strike out all four times.

It seemed that personal visits were going to be necessary.

It was 125 miles to San Diego from Los Angeles, and Booker made it in an hour and a half. He had to outrun two highway patrol cars while doing it, but in the Porsche that was no particular problem.

En route he caught a news item on the radio that mildly interested him because Margaret had asked him what he thought about the man it concerned. The newscaster said:

> *And in Washington, Secretary of State Designate Conrad Morgan goes before his final Senate subcommittee hearing this afternoon. Morgan's approval by the committee is virtually certain. At forty-one years old, Morgan will be the youngest Secretary of State during this century, if approved by the full Senate.*

Why had Margaret brought up the new Secretary of State Designate in the middle of conversation about the Black Tigers, he wondered? She had been throwing steady questions at him about the Black Tigers, then suddenly, apropos of nothing, had asked, "What do you think about Conrad Morgan being named Secretary of State Designate?"

He tried to recall what he knew of Conrad Morgan's background. The man was a career diplomat, and recently had been highly visible as Undersecretary of State, but Booker couldn't recall just what his accomplishments had been before that. He assumed that Morgan must have pretty solid credentials for the high office, or the President wouldn't have designated him, but for the life of him Booker couldn't think of what they were.

Then something jumped into his mind. Conrad Morgan had been chief delegate to the peace talks with the North Vietnamese just prior to the end of the war. Booker wondered if that had anything at all to do with Margaret's peculiarly timed question.

He had left Los Angeles at 10:30 A.M. It was only noon when he hit San Diego, but he spent another half hour getting directions to Traveltown and locating it. He pulled onto the parking lot of the amusement park at 12:30.

The park was surrounded by an iron fence eight feet high, with bars just close enough to keep out gate crashers without obstructing the view of the park from outside. Booker could see that everything inside concerned transportation. There was a stagecoach, an auto run with miniature racing cars that you could guide around a winding racecourse at up to ten miles an hour, a small-scale replica of a riverboat that circled the park in a six-foot-wide canal, an airplane ride, and an old-fashioned locomotive with a single open-sided passenger car attached to it. The railroad tracks also circled the park, alongside the canal.

Booker paid a $1.50 entrance fee, went through the gate, crossed a footbridge that spanned the canal and the railroad track, and headed for the locomotive. There was only a sprinkling of customers in the park. Two small boys were riding the racecourse, three youngsters were on the airplane ride, with their parents standing on the ground watching them go around and around, and about a dozen adults and children were taking the steamboat trip. The stagecoach, with only one pair of tired-looking horses instead of the traditional team of six, stood idle. Booker could see no one aboard the train's passenger car, which was waiting for passengers at its station.

12

Gordie Jones was polishing the brass on the near side of the engine. He wore overalls, a striped railroad man's shirt, and a blue-and-white-striped railroad cap.

Coming up behind him, Booker said, "Hi, Gordie."

The little man turned around. Physically he didn't look any different than the last time Booker had seen him, except that his mutilated ear had been somewhat repaired by plastic surgery, probably in a military hospital before he was discharged. But there was a marked change in his expression. He was no longer the vengeful young man Booker had led on commando raids. There was a simple, almost childlike innocence about him.

When Gordie spoke, Booker realized that the little man didn't recognize him. "Hey, pal, how ya doin'?" he asked cordially. "Not much business today. You doin' any?"

Booker shook his head. "No, business isn't very good."

Gordie stared at Booker with puzzlement. "You're not Sammy. How come you pretend to be Sammy?"

"It's Major Booker, Gordie. John T. Booker."

Gordie's expression of puzzlement cleared. "Oh yeah. Yeah. You do a good imitation of Sammy. You here with your kids?"

It obviously was going to do no good for Booker to try to explain who he was. He simply said, "No."

"Drivin' cars again, I bet. Huh? I bet that's what you're doin'."

Booker said, "No, Gordie, I'm not."

Gordie gestured toward the train. "I'm doin' this. I don't own it, ya know, but I'm the boss of this train. It's my uncle's. He let me drive it when I was a kid." His expression became nostalgic. "God, we used to pack 'em in."

Booker asked, "Gordie, has anyone been to see you in the last few days?"

"Oh, sure. Lotsa kids. Seventeen, maybe. Cuz, you see, we're not havin' trouble with the seagulls anymore. You like birds?"

"Some of them. Yes, I do."

"I don't like 'em all, either."

Booker said patiently, "Has anyone asked you about that last mission in Vietnam, Gordie?"

Gordie said reflectively, "What I wish we had is pelicans 'stead of seagulls."

Still patiently, Booker said, "Who asked you about the mission, Gordie?"

"Mission?"

"In Vietnam, Gordie. Remember, we were supposed to free some POWs, but they weren't there. Then the choppers never came to take us out. We had to walk out of the jungle."

Gordie looked at Booker with a flicker of recognition. "Yeah, the choppers. They never came. I know you. You took care of me in the jungle."

"That's right, Gordie," Booker said encouragingly. "I'm Major Booker. Has anybody asked you about that mission?"

Gordie nodded. "Just yesterday. A lady. Or maybe today. I told her about the pelicans. Ya know? I think she was really interested."

Booker became conscious of someone looking down at him from above. Glancing up sharply, he saw Margaret standing in the cab of the locomotive. He reached up a hand to help her down. For some moments they gazed into each other's faces while Booker still hung onto her hand.

"Who the hell *are* you?" he asked finally.

Smiling, she countered, "How was the halibut?"

"Delicious."

Gordie said, "That's what she looked like, Major." He pointed at Margaret. "The lady that came about the pelicans."

As both turned to look at him, they heard the *pfft!* of a silenced rifle from the direction of the parking lot. A red circle appeared in the center of Gordie's forehead, and he crumpled to the ground. Booker hurled Margaret to the ground.

"Stay down!" he commanded as he raced for the parking lot, weaving in order to offer a poor target.

He avoided the footbridge, instead leaping over the railroad tracks, then over the six-foot-wide canal. He cleared the exit turnstile like an Olympic hurdler and dived for the protection of the nearest parked car.

With a screech of burned rubber, a dark blue Pinto raced for the parking lot exit. It was too far away for Booker to catch the license number, and he could see nothing of the driver but the back of his head. All he could tell was that it was a man with dark hair.

By the time he reached his Porsche, the Pinto was out of sight. Booker abandoned the idea of giving pursuit and returned to the park entrance.

The gate attendant, obviously unaware of what had happened, asked curiously, "What was that all about, mister?"

Booker had no desire to be held up in San Diego by a police investigation. "Saw a guy trying to break into my car," he improvised, and continued on through the gate.

Margaret had obeyed his command to stay down, but she climbed to her feet as Booker approached. Her face was deathly pale and she gazed down at the dead man from enormous eyes. Booker knelt next to Gordie and examined the wound.

"Dammit!" he whispered. "Goddammit! I took care of you all through the war, and then you die before my eyes in a goddamn train park."

As he came to his feet a plump, middle-aged man in western dress came running over from the stagecoach. Gazing wide-eyed at the dead man, he said, "Hey, what happened to Gordie?"

"Somebody shot him," Booker said. "From the parking lot, with a silenced rifle."

The plump man looked around rather wildly. No one else in the park was looking that way. He gazed fearfully toward the parking lot.

"He took off in a dark blue Pinto," Booker said. "It was a man with black hair. I only saw him from the back, at a distance, so I can't give any other description. You can tell the police that."

"The police?"

"You're going to call them, aren't you?"

"Oh, yes, sure." The plump man hurried off toward a hotdog stand.

"Let's get the hell out of here," Booker said, taking Margaret's elbow and steering her toward the exit.

"Where?" she asked as they crossed the bridge, walking quickly, but not so fast as to attract attention.

"Guaymas, Mexico, first," Booker said. "Then Squaw Valley. Maybe I can get to Joe Walker and Mike Potter before they do."

As they pushed through the exit turnstile, the gate attendant smiled at them and said, "Hope you enjoyed your visit, folks."

"It was peachy," Booker told him.

A siren sounded in the distance as they walked across the parking lot. Margaret asked fearfully, "You think that's the cops coming already?"

"I don't know, but we're not going to wait and find out," Booker said, taking her arm and hurrying her up to a trot. When they reached the Porsche, he vaulted into the front seat, slid under the wheel and said, "Get in."

"I have my own car," she said, making no move to open the door.

"Get in before the cops get here," he said, starting the engine.

"It's rented."

"You're on an expense account."

"All my clothes are in the trunk."

"We'll get something," he said. "Goddammit, get in!"

She pulled open the door and climbed in. Booker raced the Porsche toward the exit. They had barely pulled off the lot when a police car pulled onto it.

"Close," Booker said. "You still want to go back for your goddamn clothes?"

"I'll shop in Mexico," she said. "Where is Guaymas?"

"In Sonora, on the Gulf of California. About five hundred miles as the crow flies."

"We'll drive it?"

Booker shook his head. "Take too long. I want to get there and to Squaw Valley both today, if possible."

He drove to the airport and put the Porsche in the parking lot. He got a suitcase from the car trunk.

"I see you brought your clothes," she said. "But you couldn't wait for me to get mine."

"Want me to drive you back there and drop you off?" he inquired. "If you explain to the cops that you took off only because you hate to be involved in murders, probably they won't hold you up more than a couple of days."

"Let's go check the flight schedule to Guaymas," she suggested.

There was a jet leaving in an hour. That gave them time to have some lunch, and for Booker to try to phone Mike Potter at Squaw Valley again. There still was no answer.

The flight to Guaymas would get them there at 4:00 P.M. There were no flights from Guaymas to Squaw Valley, but there was one back to San Diego at 6:00 P.M. which would get them back in time to catch a special ski flight to Squaw Valley that left San Diego at 8:00 P.M. Booker made two reservations on it.

As long as they had to wait, Margaret decided to do some shopping at the airport instead of waiting until they got to Mexico. She bought a small suitcase and filled it with new clothes and toiletry items.

It wasn't until they were on the plane that they

had a chance to talk to each other for any length of time. Both were silent during takeoff, but when the "Fasten Seat Belts" and "No Smoking" signs went off, Margaret asked, "Do you have any idea why that man was killed?"

"Uh-huh," he said.

"Why?"

He examined her in silence for a few moments. Finally he said, "I don't know enough about you. You're an unknown quantity."

"And you don't want to confide in an unknown quantity?" she asked ruefully.

"That's about it."

"Would it help if I told you my theory?" she asked.

"I'll listen, but I'm not guaranteeing I'll exchange theories."

"I think I caused it."

He looked at her with a frown. "On purpose?"

"Of course not. But I think the man who told me some things he shouldn't have at that Washington cocktail party probably told somebody else that he had told me. And that somebody else decided to take corrective action."

"How do you know that the man who talked to you didn't have second thoughts, and he's the one who is taking corrective action?"

She shook her head. "He's a harmless old man who wouldn't swat a fly. It has to be somebody else."

"Do you know who that somebody else is?"

"I have a suspicion, but I'm not at liberty to say."

"Why not? You said you're writing a book. Did you take an oath of silence with your publisher?"

"I'm just not at liberty to say."

"Then don't expect me to tell you what I know."

"Do you know anything?"

"I know why Gordie was killed. And why the other two were."

"What other two?"

He glanced at her. "You don't know everything after all, do you? Gordie was the third Black Tiger to be assassinated."

She gazed at him in shock. After a time she said, "We're going to warn Joe Walker, you said, then fly to Squaw Valley to warn Mike Potter. That means Holly Washington and Lou Goldberg must be the two you're talking about."

"You get an A in deductive logic," he said.

"And you're on the list too?"

"Naturally. Does that make a difference?"

She reached out to squeeze his hand. "You know it does."

"Enough difference to tell me everything you know?"

She released his hand. "I can't do that."

"Even if it might save my life?"

"It wouldn't help you," she said with a touch of desperation in her voice, as though trying to convince herself as much as him. "But if I can find out enough about this whole thing, maybe I can help you in another way."

"What way?"

"I can't tell you that."

"There seems to be a lot you can't tell me," he said in a bored tone. "I may as well catch a nap."

Whereupon he closed his eyes and went to sleep.

13

They landed at Guaymas on schedule at 4:00 P.M. They stored their luggage in a pay locker and Booker rented a taxicab to take them into town. The driver was a young Mexican who spoke fair English.

As they headed for the city, he asked, "Hotel, senor, or shopping plaza?"

"Neither," Booker said. "Camino del Playa."

Apparently the driver was under the impression that Americans were interested in nothing but shopping because he said in a tone of surprise, "That where fishermen live, senor. No stores there."

"Guess we'll just have to put up with that lack," Booker said. "Because that's where we want to go. Number Four-ninety-five."

"Pretty late to go out for fish," the driver said. "Or you just want to make arrange for tomorrow?"

"I don't think I follow that," Booker said.

"At that number lives American senor who run boat for rent," the driver explained. "What you call?"

"Charter boat," Margaret said.

"Sí, that it. Reason I know, American senor this morning go same place to rent boat."

Booker and Margaret looked at each other. "What did he look like?" Booker asked.

"Treinta, maybe. Big. More than sies feet. Blond, short hair. You call teamcut?"

"Crewcut," Booker said. He looked at Margaret. "Anybody you know?"

"The description rings no bell."

"Well, it could be just a tourist who likes to fish," Booker said.

Guaymas was a port town of about sixty thousand. They drove through the market section, then the driver turned toward the waterfront. Just before they got to the beach, he made a left turn onto a gravel road that ran parallel to the water.

After about a half mile they came to a row of fishing shacks strung out along the beach. Centrally located was a long floating pier with a couple of dozen individual berths. There were boats in only six of the berths, the other boats, presumably, still being out on fishing trips. A number could be seen heading for shore, as it was now about 4:30, and the fishing day was over.

"Want me to wait, senor?" the driver asked Booker.

"Yeah, do that," he said.

With Margaret trailing him, he went over to the shack numbered 495. It was a weatherbeaten building that from the outside looked as though it contained no more than two rooms. Booker rapped on the door.

When there was no answer, he tried the door, found it unlocked, and stepped inside. Margaret followed.

It did consist of only two rooms, a combination living room, dining room, and kitchen, and a bedroom, both furnished with rough, apparently handmade furniture. No one was in either room.

They went outside again and down to the pier. On one of the boats an old man sat on deck, sewing a patch on a sail.

Halting alongside the sailboat, Booker asked, "You speak English?"

"No comprender," the man said.

Margaret said, "Conocer usted Joe Walker?"

"Sí. Yo conocer vista Senor Walker."

Margaret turned to Booker. "He says he knows him by sight. Aren't you glad you brought me along?"

"I could have used the taxi driver as an interpreter. Ask him if he knows where Joe is?"

Margaret and the old man had considerable conversation in Spanish. The old man peered out to sea, then they had some more conversation.

Eventually she said to Booker, "He says Walker took an American tourist out fishing this morning. Big, blond, and with a crewcut. None of those boats coming in are Walker's."

A number of boats were now getting close. They waited until the first one docked, then went over to it. It was a thirty-foot launch with twin inboard motors, manned by a small, dark, wiry man in his thirties and a thick-bodied man in his fifties.

"You fellows speak English?" Booker asked.

The younger one said, "Me. Not my father."

"You know Joe Walker?"

"Sí."

"You see him out there today?"

The man nodded. "He still trolling about five mile out. Got some American aboard."

"When's he usually come in?"

The little man shrugged. "American tourists like to get money's worth. Sometimes almost dark." He looked up at the sun. "That about seven this time of year."

Booker said, "For twenty bucks would you take us out to him?"

The man looked interested. After a brief conversation with the older man, he said, "Sure, come aboard."

Margaret and Booker clambered aboard. The

boat was full of nets and fishing rods and boxes full of freshly caught fish, but they managed to find room to sit on the benches running along each side. Booker sat on one side and Margaret on the other in order to balance the boat.

Booker handed the wiry little man a twenty-dollar bill. He in turn handed it to his father, who stuck it in his pocket. The younger man started the engines, backed from the berth, swung the bow seaward, and opened the throttle.

The twin engines were diesel, and were of high horsepower. They skimmed over the water at a speed Booker estimated to be at least forty knots. In a matter of minutes they came in sight of a becalmed thirty-five-foot cabin cruiser.

"There it is," the wiry skipper shouted above the noise of the engines.

He cut the speed and drifted to within twenty feet of the other boat. The only person visible aboard was a tall blond man of about thirty in a blue jacket. He was at the helm, seemingly trying to start the engine. When the launch came near, he stepped down from the cabin onto the deck and came over to the rail.

"Am I glad to see you," he said. "I can't get this thing going."

Both Booker and Margaret had stood up and were standing by the rail nearest the other boat. Booker asked, "Where's Joe Walker?"

"I guess he drowned," the blond man said. "He fell overboard trying to net a sailfish I hooked. I swung back to look for him, but I'm not very good at handling a boat, and I'm not sure I got back to the same place. Walker had spiked the wheel, and the boat ran on its own for some distance before I got to the wheel."

Booker stared at the man for some time, then

turned to the little skipper of the launch. "You think Joe Walker would fall overboard trying to boat a fish?"

The little man shook his head. "No way. Something fishy here."

"Yes," Booker agreed. He faced the blond man again. "I'm John Booker, you son-of-a-bitch," he said softly. "You're going to have a man-overboard accident too." Again he turned back to the wiry little man. "Pull in next to that boat."

The blond man reached inside his jacket and drew out a lemon-shaped metal object. Pulling its pin, he casually tossed it over into the launch, then dropped flat.

Catching it, Booker tossed it back, yelled, "Hit the deck!" hurled Margaret down, and fell on top of her.

The wiry little man grabbed his father and fell on top of him just as the grenade went off in the other boat. With his ears ringing, Booker climbed to his feet and looked over at the cabin cruiser. He couldn't see below the near rail, but he could see blood spattered all over the far one.

Margaret and the two owners of the launch also climbed to their feet. The owners peered over the side to see if their boat had suffered any damage. It hadn't, because the rail of the other boat had prevented grenade fragments from coming their way. The entire force of the explosion had been directed upward.

Margaret was deathly pale. Booker put a steadying arm about her waist.

"Better sit down with your back to the other boat," he suggested. "I'm going to have them pull in so I can go aboard. And that blond guy's not gonna be a pretty sight."

"Why do you want to go aboard?" she asked unsteadily.

"It's just possible he lied, and Joe's tied up down below." He turned to the little skipper. "Can you pull in right next to Walker's boat?"

Nodding, the little man returned to the wheel, shifted into gear, and slid the launch alongside the other boat. His father grabbed the other boat's rail to hold the two boats together.

Booker jumped over onto the other deck, landing alongside of the remains of the blond man. The grenade had exploded right next to him, and he was spread about in pieces.

There was no way to avoid stepping in blood, but Booker did manage to avoid stepping on any severed limbs en route to the hatch leading below. Down below there was a small galley and a cabin with double bunks on both sides. No one was there.

Going topside again, Booker jumped back onto the other boat and signaled the skipper's father to let go. As they drifted away from the cabin cruiser, he said to the little man, "Think there's any point in circling around to see if we can find Walker?"

"That fellow, he kill him before he throw him in water," the little man said positively. "We look around if you want, though."

"Probably be better if we just informed the coast guard, or whatever you call it here. They could get helicopters on it."

The little man nodded. "I could call them—how you say, meaning secret?"

"Anonymously," Margaret said.

"Right. That word."

"Do you also plan to make any kind of report to the regular police?" Booker asked.

"Do you?" the skipper countered.

"We could just slide back in and pretend we'd never been out here," Booker suggested.

"That would save involvement with the policia," the man agreed. "But for our trouble—"

When he let it trail off, Booker took out another twenty and handed it to him.

"Gracias, senor," he said, beaming. He relayed the bill to his father, who stuck it in his pocket.

They returned to port at the same speed at which they had come out. It was only shortly after five when they docked.

The cab was still waiting. They returned to the airport, arriving fifteen minutes before flight time. They had no conversation en route, because of the presence of the cab driver. They waited until they were aloft in the plane, heading back to San Diego, before they discussed Walker's death.

Then Margaret asked, "How were you so that man had murdered Walker?"

"With a contract out on Joe, it would have been mighty coincidental for him to die accidentally. Particularly in the clumsy way Blondie said. Joe looked awkward, but he was better coordinated than anyone else I ever knew. He wasn't the kind of guy to fall overboard."

After a period of silence, she said, "Wouldn't it have been helpful to find out who that blond man was? I suppose it would have been messy, but maybe you should have looked at his identification papers."

"They would have been faked," Booker said. "He was a Company hit man."

"What kind of hit man?"

"Scratch that," Booker said. "I shouldn't have said it."

14

At the San Diego Airport Booker again tried Mike Potter's number at Squaw Valley. This time a woman answered the phone.

"Mike there?" Booker asked.

"He's still out on ski patrol."

"Oh. Is this his wife?"

She chuckled. "You don't know Mike very well, do you?"

"As a matter of fact I do," Booker said. "We just haven't been in touch lately. What did I say that's funny?"

"Mike's a confirmed bachelor. I should know. I've been trying to change that status for three years."

"Well, I wish you luck. I'm John Booker, and I'm calling from San Diego."

"Major John Booker?" she asked.

"Formerly Major."

"Sure, he talks about you a lot, Major. I'm sort of a next-door neighbor. Only up here neighbors are a mile apart. I'm Judy Webb."

"How are you, Judy? I take it you're a, ah, close friend of Mike's."

"The only way we could get closer is to be married. Reason I'm here when he's not, is I have a key."

"I see. Will you give him a message?"

"Sure, Major. Shoot."

"I'm catching an eight-o'clock plane to Squaw Valley. I'll phone him soon as I arrive. Meantime, tell him it's Code Red."

"Code Red? What does that mean?"

"He'll know," Booker told her. "Just give him the message."

"Okay, Major. But about phoning him when you get in, he may not be here. Reason he isn't home now is some idiot got himself lost. Mike just called that he's been spotted stranded on a ledge up on the north slope. He's coming home for dinner, but then he has to go out again to help get the idiot down. If it's a moonlit night, so they can see to work, he may be gone half the night."

"I'll try him anyway when I get there," Booker said.

Booker and Margaret were the only two on the plane from San Diego to Squaw Valley who were not in ski clothes. About half of the passengers were young, probably most of them college students, but there was an equal number of middle-aged skiers.

"I feel out of place," Margaret whispered to Booker as they taxied for takeoff. "I should have bought a ski suit while I was shopping."

"Then they'd only wonder why I'm not in one," he whispered back. "Don't worry about it. They'll think we're old pros. They'll think we ski so often we keep our outfits and skis up there."

Shortly after they were in flight, Booker rose to go back to the bathroom. Since he and Margaret had seats at the front of the plane, this gave him opportunity to look over all the other passengers.

On the right toward the rear a middle-aged Oriental man with graying hair, a mustache, and thick glasses was seated by the window, next to a young college student who had settled back with closed eyes to go to sleep. As Booker approached, the man took a handkerchief from his pocket and sneezed into it.

Booker probably would have paid no attention to the man, but he got the peculiar impression that the sneeze was forced, leading him to the suspicion that the man was simply using the handkerchief as an excuse to shield his face from Booker. With a contract out on him, Booker was automatically suspicious of any stranger who did anything whatever out of the ordinary. He therefore looked at him more closely than he would have if the man had not sneezed.

Although the lower part of the Oriental's face was shielded by the handkerchief, the upper part was visible. Booker couldn't think of any Oriental he had ever known who wore such thick glasses and had gray hair. When he got to the bathroom, he searched his memory, but no one seemed to fit.

His trip to the bathroom had been solely to check out the other passengers. After waiting a few moments, he returned. He moved back along the aisle slowly, attempting to get a glimpse of the Oriental man's profile as he passed. But the man seemed to sense his approach, and turned his face away as though he were engrossed with the view out the window as Booker passed by.

The ploy, if it was a ploy, was a failure. As it was now dark, the window acted as a mirror, and Booker was able to get a full front view of his face reflected in the window. He had no recollection of ever having seen it before.

When he got back to his seat, he spent some time wondering why the man had gone to such pains to avoid letting Booker see his face, when he was an utter stranger. Of course if he was a hit man from the Company, it was possible that it had simply been nervousness at seeing his potential victim face-to-face. But that hardly seemed in character for a Company hit man. Generally they had no nerves.

Probably his imagination had simply become overactive, Booker thought, and he was reading too much into perfectly normal actions.

Still the man made him uneasy. Turning to Margaret, he said brusquely, "Go to the bathroom."

Margaret looked at him strangely. "Number one or two?" she asked with sarcasm.

In a less authoritative tone he said, "The window seat, third row from the back, right side as you go down the aisle. An Oriental. See if you recognize him."

Obediently rising to her feet, Margaret moved along the aisle to the rear of the plane. She glanced at the Oriental as she went by, he gave her a quick glance, as though taking a mental picture, then turned his head to sneeze into his handkerchief. She continued on to the bathroom.

When she came back and slipped into her seat, she said to Booker, "Looks like a waiter at a Chinese restaurant I used to frequent in Des Moines."

Booker hiked an eyebrow at her. "I'll bet the Chinese food in Des Moines is something to remember."

"Is he following us?" she asked.

"I'm not sure. Maybe I'm being over-imaginative, but I got the impression he was trying to hide his face from me as I went by."

"So did I. But it could be he's just shy, and tries to hide his face from everybody. Or it could be that waiter. I don't think I tipped him the last time I was in."

Beneath her flipness, Booker realized she was frightened. He reached over to squeeze her hand. She held onto it tightly and looked into his face.

"Will you take care of me if it is that waiter?" she asked.

"I'll take care of you no matter who it is," he assured her.

"Even if it's another Company hit man?"

He made no answer to that.

"I've been thinking," she said. "Isn't 'The Company' the inside name CIA agents use for the CIA?"

"What makes you think I know anything about the CIA?" he countered.

"It came out in the Senate investigation of the CIA that they've pulled some assassinations," Margaret said. "But of people in foreign countries. Have they taken to killing American citizens in their own country now?"

"You're developing an overactive imagination too," he told her. "Who did you talk to at that cocktail party in Washington?"

"Please don't ask," she said, squeezing his hand. "I'm pretty sure I'll lie."

They landed at the airport at Squaw Valley a little after nine-thirty. As they moved with the other passengers toward the terminal, Booker was conscious of the Oriental man following only a short distance behind them. When they reached the terminal, Booker steered Margaret over to a bank of pay telephones.

"Make a call," he said, pushing her into a booth.

"To who?" she asked, confused.

"It's to whom?" he corrected. "To nobody. You're just pretending, stupid."

"Oh." She closed the booth door, lifted the receiver and pretended to drop a coin in the slot.

Booker stood facing the booth, watching the line of passengers go by, reflected in the glass of the booth. The Oriental went by without a glance their way.

Pushing the booth door open, Booker said, "Okay."

Margaret stepped from the booth and both of them looked after the Oriental man. A middle-aged Oriental woman approached him and gave him a restrained embrace, in the reserved fashion of the Far East.

"Just an ordinary guy being met by his wife," Margaret said in a tone of relief.

"Yeah, I guess so," Booker said dubiously, wanting to buy it, but still not quite convinced.

The Oriental man had already recovered his baggage and was moving toward the terminal exit with the woman who had met him when Booker and Margaret arrived at the baggage room. The baggage from their flight had already come down the chute. They picked out their suitcases. Then Booker led the way over to a car rental desk.

"Any Porsches?" he asked the female clerk.

"Oh, no sir. No sports cars up here. Gets too cold at night. I can give you a nice Cobra two-door."

"All right," Booker agreed, not particular so long as there were no Porsches.

After he filled out the proper forms, the girl gave him the car keys and told him where to find the car on the parking lot. As Booker loaded their luggage into the car trunk, he noticed a blue Celica with two people in it two lanes away. Constantly alert to danger now, the only reason he noticed them was that they were sitting so quietly.

From that distance, and in the dark, he couldn't make out their faces, but he had a strange feeling that they were the Oriental couple who had walked out of the terminal at least ten minutes previously.

He kept his eye on the Celica as he backed from the parking slot and headed for the exit. Periodically he glanced into the rear-view mirror to see if it was following until he got to the exit gate. When it hadn't moved by then, he decided his imagination was still being overactive.

Reservations on the ski flight had included reservations at the Squaw Valley Inn also. It was some miles from the airport, along a winding mountain road. Booker drove the first part of it in silence, thinking. Margaret alternately gazed at him curiously, and at the moonlit view of the mountains.

"Your friend must be climbing up to that ledge," she said finally. "It's bright enough."

Booker merely grunted.

"When you're silent, you're silent," Margaret said. "Tell me what you're thinking."

"Old friends," Booker said briefly.

He still couldn't place the Oriental man's face, but it crept into his mind that something about that false sneeze was familiar. He probed for it, but it kept escaping him, like a word on the tip of the tongue that won't quite materialize.

Then it suddenly hit him. He and Mhin Van Thieu were walking along a main street in Saigon when a Vietnamese woman Mhin apparently recognized, but didn't want to recognize him, turned the corner ahead of them and came their way. Out came the handkerchief, there was the false sneeze into it, with the handkerchief covering his face until they were by, then Mhin put away the handkerchief and continued on as though nothing had happened.

Mentally Booker stripped away the thick glasses and mustache of the Oriental on the plane and took the gray from his hair. The much younger man beneath the disguise was easily identifiable.

"Mhin!" he said aloud.

15

"Huh?" Margaret said.

"That Oriental man on the plane was Mhin."

"Oh, ho!" Margaret said in a sinister tone, twisting an imaginary mustache like the villain of a nineteenth-century melodrama. "Major Mhin Van Thieu. Another Black Tiger. The plot thickens."

Booker looked at her sharply. "What don't you know?"

Margaret shrugged.

"What did you talk to him about?" Booker asked.

"Mhin? I've never said a word to him in my life."

"Murray Saunders."

"Murray Saunders? I don't know any Murray Saunders."

Booker suddenly swerved the car off the road to park on the shoulder. He did it simply because he wanted some serious talk without the distraction of driving, but by pure accident the maneuver also disclosed that they had a tail. They had just rounded a blind curve before he pulled over, and the following car wasn't aware of that until it was too late to pull over behind them. The blue Celica went past.

Booker gazed after it until it rounded another curve ahead. It had been too dark to see who was in the car, but he was certain it was the disguised Mhin and the Oriental woman who had met him at the airport.

What was Mhin's game, he wondered? Was he on Booker's side, or was he working for the CIA? His memory jumped back to the time Murray Saunders had visited him in the Saigon military hospital. Saunders had said, "The brass thinks maybe Major Mhin Van Thieu was a double agent."

Had he been? Booker wondered. And if he had, wasn't it more likely that the CIA would have assassinated him long ago instead of using him as an agent? After reflection he decided it wasn't necessarily more likely. The CIA had a habit of capitalizing on weaknesses by using people. It was quite possible that they had simply used the knowledge that Mhin had been a double agent to blackmail him into working for them.

Booker had assumed that Mhin was on the CIA Sanction Authorized list simply because his name and address was on the computer printout that Murray Saunders had handed him. But in thinking back, Booker couldn't recall that Saunders had actually said he was. As a matter of fact, now that he thought about it, the CIA agent's implication had been that he was not.

Saunders' words had been: "It's not just you. A funny rumor seeped to me a while back that something was brewing about the Black Tigers. That gave me a reason to check out all five of the other guys who came out of the jungle with you. There's contracts on all of you."

All five of the other guys who came out of the jungle with you, Saunders had said. No mention of Mhin Van Thieu.

Margaret interrupted his train of thought by saying, "Is something the matter? Are you ill?"

Jerked back to the present, Booker looked at her. "Just thinking about Mhin. If my guess is right, he and that woman who met him were in that blue Celica that just passed."

"They were following us, you think?"

"Uh-huh."

"It was clever of you to catch them at it by pulling over."

"Accident," Booker said. "I didn't know we were being tailed. I pulled over because I wanted to talk to you."

"Oh?" she said interestedly. "Can't you wait until we get to the hotel?"

"Can the humor for a while," he said irritably. "You were someone named Marilyn Cook."

When she gazed at him blankly, he said, "You told Murray you were Marilyn Cook of the *Los Angeles Times*."

"Oh, *that* Murray Saunders."

"What did he tell you?"

"Nothing."

Booker studied her broodingly, not believing her. "I want to know who you met at that cocktail party, and I want to know what he told you."

She shook her head. "I told you I couldn't."

"Do you give a damn about me?" he demanded.

She looked at him steadily. "I'm crazy about you."

"Then you're going to have to weigh your

loyalties. Is your oath of silence to whoever the hell you're working for worth seeing me dead?"

"Don't do this to me," she protested.

"Why the hell not? I'm fighting for my life. Make up your mind fast."

There was a long period of silence, ending with a resigned sigh from Margaret. "He was a government official," she said.

"Who?"

"That doesn't matter. He's an old man. He's retiring. He was a pawn. All that's important is that he indicated to me there was something that wasn't kosher about that mission."

"What?"

" 'Secret,' he said."

"Secret what?"

"He was drunk. He just kept repeating: 'Secret, secret.' I did the rest myself."

"And what did you come up with?"

"Only a suspicion about what might have happened, and who may have made it happen. No proof. Not even convincing evidence. There's no way I could tell you that."

"Why not?"

"Because it's the sort of thing that if I'm wrong, the rumor could ruin a career. I can't risk that. It isn't because I've pledged silence to anyone. It's a matter of personal ethics. I just can't."

"You think I'd spread the rumor?"

"No, but you talk in your sleep."

"That's ridiculous," he said.

"Well, I'm stuck with it, so you'll have to make the best of it. I've told you all I intend to, John. And that was more than I should have."

Her tone was so definite that he knew there was no point in pressing the matter further. He shifted into drive and continued on.

When they pulled onto the parking lot of the Squaw Valley Inn, Booker carefully looked over all the other cars on the lot. There was no blue Celica parked there.

"Guess they're staying somewhere else," he said as he unlocked the trunk to get their luggage.

"Who?" she asked, shivering in the cold because she had on only a light jacket.

Booker, wearing only a suit coat, felt the cold too. "Mhin and his female friend," he said.

"Are you sure that was Mhin?" she asked.

"Certain."

"Why would he be in disguise?"

"Either to hide from the CIA, or because he didn't want me to recognize him. I lean toward the latter. If he was on our side, seems to me he would have given me some kind of signal to identify himself."

"Maybe he couldn't because somebody else was watching both of you," she suggested.

Slamming the trunk lid and picking up both suitcases, he said, "That's a pleasant thought. Now I can worry about the other passengers on the plane."

Hurrying to keep up with him as he strode toward the inn, she said, "We should have brought coats. We'll freeze up here."

"I'm sure there'll be a shop," he said. "We'll pick up some ski clothes in the morning."

At the registration desk Booker gave his name to the young woman clerk and said, "Reservation for two."

After checking a list, she said, "Yes, sir," and handed him a registration card. "Twin beds or double, sir?"

"Double," Margaret said before Booker could answer.

When he finished filling out the registration card, the girl glanced at it, then snapped a clicker for a bellhop. As a uniformed bellhop approached, the clerk said, "You got here just in time, Mr. Booker."

"For what?" he asked.

"Snow's melting fast."

The bellhop reached the desk. The woman clerk handed him two keys and said, "Room Two-twenty-two."

As the bellhop picked up the two suitcases, Booker said to Margaret, "You go on up. I want to make a phone call."

"You just want me to give the tip," she said darkly, following after the bellhop.

"You know Mike Potter?" Booker asked the girl behind the desk.

"Sure. He's on the ski patrol. Right now he's up at the north slope, trying to rescue some guy off a ledge a couple of thousand feet up."

"He's still out?"

"Well, I wouldn't know that. Want to try his house?"

"Yes," Booker said. "Where's the phone?"

"We don't have a pay phone. Phone company took it out because nobody ever used it. I'll dial it for you."

She dialed a number and handed the phone to Booker. It rang ten times before he hung it up.

"You know Judy Webb?" he asked.

"Sure," she said. "She's been trying to net Mike for three years."

There was a touch of jealousy in her voice, which, combined with her having dialed Potter's number without having to look it up, suggested that she had ideas about netting the bachelor herself.

"Could you dial her number for me?"

The girl silently dialed the number and handed the phone to Booker again. There was no answer there either. After ten rings he hung up.

"Probably she's delivering coffee to the rescue team," the clerk said disdainfully. "Little Miss Goodheart. But she only does it when Mike's part of the team."

"How tough would it be to go out there?" Booker asked.

She examined his suitcoat and necktie. "You'd need warmer clothes, skis, a guide, and a couple of hours. Then, when you got there, Mike might be up on the ledge. If you can wait till tomorrow, there'll be no problem. He's jump crazy. He'll be on the jump first thing in the morning, even if he's been up all night."

"Guess I'll wait, then," Booker said. "Thanks for all your trouble."

Booker found the door to Room 222 unlocked. As he went in and locked the door behind him, Margaret came from the bathroom drying her wet skin with a towel.

"To what extent are we speaking to each other?" she asked.

He looked at her. "What do you want to talk about?"

She finished drying herself, tossed the towel over the back of a chair, and stood there naked. "Well, I was wondering, for instance, if we're speaking enough to share the only bed in the room."

Booker shrugged. "Sure, we can share the bed."

She pulled down the covers and climbed into the double bed. Undressing, Booker hung up his suit, tossed the dirty laundry on the closet floor, and went into the bathroom. Margaret heard the shower turn on. She switched on the bedlamp, got up to turn off the room light, and climbed back into bed again.

Ten minutes later he came from the bathroom nude, leaving the bathroom door open and the bathroom light on.

"Switch out that light," he ordered.

Obediently she reached up to switch out the bed-lamp. The glow from the bathroom dimly lighted the room, but it was dark over by the window. Booker moved over to it and peered out.

Margaret said, "Well, here I am in the only bed in the room."

Booker took one last glance out the window, then walked over to seat himself on the side of the bed next to her.

"Any enemies out there?" she asked.

"I'm just as worried about the enemy within," he said, gazing down at her contemplatively. "Are you an enemy, Margaret?"

"No."

"After that cocktail party, were you in Chicago and New York?"

"Ugly cities. Why would I be either place?"

"Chicago is where Holly Washington was assassinated and New York is where Lou Goldberg disappeared. You just happened to be there when Gordie Jones was killed today. Ditto when Joe Walker got it. Were you there when Holly and Lou got it, too?"

Staring up at him with a wounded expression in her eyes, she shook her head no.

He said, "You certainly didn't resist flying down to look for Joe, or coming up here to look for Mike. Are you some kind of finger man for who-ever's doing this?"

"Finger person," she corrected.

Booker didn't smile. She reached out to take his hand. "John, I haven't lied to you."

Booker began to melt. "Including last night?" he asked.

"Especially last night."

Booker slipped under the covers next to her. Pulling her against him, he said against her lips, "A beautiful woman of mystery. You fit in somewhere."

"So do you," she said with a little gasp.

16

In the morning Booker and Margaret went downstairs to breakfast in the hotel coffee shop. Booker asked their waitress when activity usually started at the ski jump.

"The first tram starts up at nine," the waitress said. "You've got lots of time. It isn't even eight yet."

After breakfast they visited the wing of the hotel devoted to shops. In a clothing store both bought ski suits and ski boots. As they emerged from the clothing store with their packages, Margaret stopped to look into the window of a sporting goods store. Booker halted also and gave her an inquiring look.

"Should we buy skis?" she asked.

"For what? We're going to get out of here as soon as we contact Mike Potter."

"Just thought we might make a vacation of it."

He gazed at her. "I'm dodging a hit, and you want to make a vacation out of it?"

"Don't get sore," she said. "It was only a suggestion. There is also the factor that everybody is going to look at us strangely if we get on that tram without skis."

"If anyone from the hit team is on the tram, our carrying skis isn't going to fool him. As for buying skis just to avoid embarrassment, screw it. You know what a good set of skis costs?"

"That was only a suggestion too," Margaret said. "Don't be such an old grouch."

They carried their packages to their room and changed into their ski clothes. Booker, who had not shaved before breakfast, went into the bathroom to do that after dressing. Margaret switched on the room's TV set.

"Hey!" she called to Booker in the bathroom. "The Senate confirmation hearings for Conrad Morgan are on live."

"Peachy-dandy," he called back sardonically through the open door.

Margaret sat on the end of the bed to watch the hearings. The committee chairman was saying:

> *Once again, Mr. Morgan, I want to thank you for the cooperation you are affording the committee in your appearance here today.*

The Secretary of State Designate said:

> *Well, thank you, Senator. I want to assure you and the other members of the committee that I understand the necessity for hearings such as these, and I want you to feel free to*

probe any areas at all that might be of interest to you.

"Big of you," Margaret muttered to herself. The committee chairman said:

I'm sure I speak for the entire committee, sir, when I say that an attitude such as that is deeply appreciated. We've all had experience with other kinds of witnesses.

Booker stepped to the bathroom door, wiping residual shaving cream from his face with a wet washcloth. Eyeing the screen with a somewhat jaundiced eye, he asked, "Think he'll make it?"

"Morgan? Oh, yes. He's the new darling of Washington."

Conrad Morgan was saying:

Well, I know just what you mean, Senator. I've dealt with that type many times myself.

The chairman said:

I'm sure you have. Now then, Mr. Morgan, let us begin by discussing the recent unpleasantness in Vietnam.

"Unpleasantness, he calls it," Booker growled. "What the hell would he call a nuclear war? A squabble?"

"Shhh," Margaret said. "I want to hear this."

Booker reentered the bathroom. The committee chairman asked:

What could you do, as Secretary of State, to guard against a repetition of that kind of involvement by the United States?

Morgan said:

> *Well, Senator, I'm sure you're aware that*
> *the attitude of the nation is far different today*
> *from what it was in the days before Vietnam.*
> *The American people today are far less eager*
> *to become involved in foreign adventures of*
> *doubtful advantage, and I, of course, tend to*
> *share that point of view.*

Booker came from the bathroom, smelling of
bay rum. "We better get going," he said.

The chairman of the Senate committee said:

> *Of course. But if the strategic position of*
> *the United States at some time in the future*
> *called for the use of armed force, would you*
> *be willing to—*

The rest was cut off because Booker turned off
the set. "We have five minutes to make the tram,"
he said.

She got up and followed him from the room.

The tram boarding station was alongside the
hotel. The seats of the single car were already full
of colorfully dressed skiers, and standees were now
boarding. Booker and Margaret crowded on last.
Despite Margaret's fears of arousing attention because they had no skis or poles, no one seemed to
notice their lack.

The tram operator, a young man of college age,
looked toward the hotel's front door and asked
generally, "Anyone know if anybody else is coming?"

Booker said, "We were last out, and didn't see
anyone else in the lobby in ski clothes."

"Then hang on ladies and gentlemen, because h-e-e-r-e we go!"

After that dramatic announcement, the car pulled away rather sedately and began to move upward along the stretched steel cables toward the mountaintop ski runs.

The operator said, "For the benefit of newcomers, the Squaw Valley Inn is at three thousand feet above sea level. The top of the ski run we are climbing to is at eight thousand feet, or nearly a mile above the valley. The jump at the bottom of the slide is a hundred feet above the ground. For those inexperienced in jumping, there are alternate ski runs on either side of the jump that may be taken. There are also escape paths from the center run, just before you reach the top of the jump slide, in case you have a last-minute change of mind."

Booker looked over the crowd of passengers, trying to divine if any of them were members of the CIA hit team. He glanced only briefly at the college-age skiers, figuring that the CIA would be unlikely to hire killers that young. Among the others he was able to pick out no one who didn't look like an ordinary vacationer.

At least Mhin wasn't among the group, he thought. Which allowed him to concentrate on danger from other directions.

The tram operator pointed off to the left at a towering mountain and said, "That is Sleeping Princess Mountain, so named because if you have enough imagination, it's supposed to look like the head and torso of an Indian maiden lying on her back. I've never been able to see it myself, but you're all welcome to try. This side of the mountain is known as the north slope, and is famous for mountain climbing mishaps. Can you see that dark line running across the face of the slope about a third of the way up?"

There was a general murmur indicating that the passengers could.

"That's a ledge where climbers rest on the way up, or camp if an unexpected storm comes up. Last night an amateur climber got stranded up there, and I understood it took the ski patrol until three in the morning to get him down."

By then they were arriving at the station at the top. The tram slid up to the concrete platform smoothly, the doors opened, and the skiers disembarked. They all began to put on their skis. Booker and Margaret tarried on the platform to look around carefully in all directions. Aside from the skiers who had come with them, no one was in sight. But then, up a steep road on the opposite side of the mountain from the tram lift, a snowmobile roared. It came to a halt next to a ski shack of corrugated iron and the driver jumped down.

He was a tall, lean, hard-bodied man in a bright red ski suit. The ski shack was only about fifty-yards from the tram platform, but Booker and Margaret couldn't make out his features because he wore a ski mask. He lifted a pair of skis from the snowmobile and knelt to tie them on.

"That could be Mike," Booker said. "He's built like that."

As he and Margaret moved in that direction, the man rose and skied over the top of the ski run.

Skiers were lining up at the top of each of the three runs when Booker and Margaret got over there. Booker tapped the man in the red ski suit on the shoulder.

When the man turned around, Booker said, "I'm looking for Mike Potter."

"You've got him, Major," the man said, pulling

off his ski mask and grinning at Booker. "What
the hell you doin' here?"

17

A starter, also in a red ski suit, came over to in-
struct the skiers on the rules. As he passed by he
said to Potter, "You going down, Mike?"

"In a minute," Potter said. "I'm greeting an old
friend." He looked at Margaret curiously.

"Margaret Cash, Mike," Booker said. "Margaret,
this is Mike Potter."

They told each other they were glad to meet
each other. Then Potter asked again, "What you
doin' here, Major?"

"Your father sent me with a bag of chili. He
wants to make up."

"Right," Mike said, nodding with mock serious-
ness. "Well, tell him one of us has to change his
lifestyle. You up here on vacation?"

"Didn't you get my message?"

In an amused voice Potter said, "You mean about
Code Red, Major? I thought it was a gag."

"It wasn't." Booker gestured toward the corrugated iron shack. "Let's go in there. We have to
talk."

Laughing, Potter said, "Come on, what is this?"

"Mike, you and I are both in acute danger. We're
the only two left of the Black Tigers. Somebody's
wiping them out. Holly, Lou, Gordie, and Mike are
already dead."

"The hell you say!" Potter said, shocked.

"We've got to talk, Mike."

The starter called, "You're up, Mike."

"Okay, we'll talk," Potter said. "Meet me at the bottom. You know how some people can't get moving in the morning until they've had a cup of coffee? Well, I don't come fully awake until I've have a jump."

Margaret said, "Then why didn't you stay home in bed with your girl friend?"

Potter looked at her and burst out laughing. "Not that kind of jump."

"I think we ought to get out of the open," Booker said.

"Meet me at the bottom," Potter repeated, and poled himself over into the starting box.

At the starter's signal, Potter poled himself over the edge of the run and started downward. His skis sliding in the tracks of previous skiers, he rapidly picked up speed. Crouched low to lessen wind resistance, he reached the end of the ramp at full speed, lifted off, and stretched out into a perfect jump angle.

Gracefully he soared through the air, reaching far, far out. Then suddenly, a rifle shot rang out, echoing through the mountains. Potter maintained his perfect form for the space of a heartbeat, then slowly began to lose shape until his tumbling body smashed into the snow-covered jump landing, staining it blood red. The body continued down the hillside, arms and legs akimbo, shattered skis snapping into the air like toothpicks.

The echoing mountains ringing the valley made it impossible to tell from which direction the shot had come. But on the principle that the sniper would undoubtedly pick him as the next target, Booker grabbed Margaret's arm and rushed her toward the parked snowmobile, intending to take cover behind it.

The rifle sounded again, just as they reached it, and the left headlight of the snowmobile exploded in a shower of shattered glass. Then Booker was hurling Margaret flat and diving into the snow next to her.

Skiers were scurrying for cover inside and behind the ski shack. A middle-aged skier crouched alongside the shack pointed to the hillside just south of them and yelled, "I saw a puff of smoke right there!"

Peering that way, Booker saw a figure in a white ski suit and matching ski mask, carrying a rifle, burst from a stand of trees halfway up the hillside and begin running down the slope for the road leading to the Squaw Valley Inn. The point at which the running figure would reach the road was a good half mile from the hotel, and close to a quarter mile from the group at the bottom of the jump that was converging on the broken body of Mike Potter.

Even assuming that anyone in that group would be brave enough to chase after a killer with a rifle, no one would have been able to get there before the killer reached the road. And no doubt an escape vehicle was parked conveniently nearby.

Booker jumped onto the seat of the snowmobile, kicked the engine alive and twisted the throttle wide open. The snowmobile lunged toward the jump gate and over the edge of the center run.

Booker kept the throttle wide open as the snowmobile accelerated along the steep incline in a frightening rush toward the end of the ramp and the yawning wide-open space beyond the end of the drop-off. He was probably traveling at 120 miles per hour when the vehicle reached the edge and took off in a great leap through the air, the rear treads spinning wildly when there was suddenly nothing but air beneath them for traction.

The snowmobile soared over the group around Mike Potter's body, those on the ground gazing up at it openmouthed. Two hundred feet beyond the end of the ramp it touched down into the snow in a great sliding, yawing crunch, and it was another hundred feet before the spinning treads gained traction. Then, engine roaring, it barreled the rest of the way down the hill.

The running sniper had reached the road while the snowmobile was still roaring through the air. Then he turned left and raced along the shoulder a few yards to where a motorcycle was concealed in the underbrush alongside the road. The sniper had heard the roaring engine of the snowmobile, but he had been too intent on avoiding a tumble in the ankle-deep snow to look that way, and was unaware of its dramatic flight from the end of the jump ramp. Snowmobiles were so common in that area that the sniper paid the sound little attention.

The sniper had pulled apart the high-powered rifle into two pieces while running, and now shoved the disassembled pieces into a special compartment beneath the gas tank before vaulting onto the seat. Quickly kick-starting the engine, the killer sped away.

As Booker rode through the center of the base ski area, people who were running from the hotel toward the crowd surrounding Mike Potter's body scattered out of his way. Booker revved the engine, then slowed for a moment as he scanned the area. From shortly beyond where the sniper had disappeared around a curve in the road, he heard the motorcycle start and gun away.

There was no way he could chase the motorcycle along the highway, because the snowmobile was built to travel on snow, and the road had been cleared by snowplows. But he recalled from the trip in from the airport to the hotel that the road had a long, sweeping curve to the left a few hundred yards beyond the point from which the motorcycle had started. Fortunately that was on the high side of the road. The right side was edged by a steep drop-off.

Heading for the knoll from which the sniper had fired, Booker gunned up it, over the top, and down the other side. Cutting off an angle away from the road, he sped around and in between trees, up and over more knolls, sometimes plowing through thick underbrush that tore at his clothing when there was no open route, sometimes roaring across small gullies at high speed.

The sniper, riding at equally high speed along the twisting highway, looked back to see if anyone was following. The road was empty behind. Off to the left there was the roaring noise of some kind of engine, but it was far enough away so that the motorcyclist assumed it was on some other road. Since the sound seemed to recede steadily as though the vehicle were moving away, the sniper dismissed it as a possible threat.

The cyclist throttled down to a less headlong speed, now confident of a flawless getaway. The motorcycle had been rounding a long, sweeping curve for some time. Now the road straightened out and the straightaway ahead was clear as far as the cyclist could see.

Then a snowmobile slid down the snow-covered bank on the left side of the road and came to a halt, blocking the entire left lane. A muscular figure in a ski suit leaped from the vehicle to stand in the center of the other lane, hands on hips.

The sniper's motorcycle roared straight at the motionless figure. The man in the ski suit remained motionless until the last second. Then he jumped to the left, leaped high into the air, and snapped out both legs in a powerful thrust-kick.

The cyclist was caught in the neck and left side. The double kick lifted the rider from the seat to sail across the road and over the edge of the steep drop-off on the right. Spinning out of control, the motorcycle roared over the edge too, crashing onto the rocks fifty feet below and bursting into flames.

Booker climbed down the steep bank to the twisted body lying on the rocks. The motorcycle was burning briskly another twenty-five yards beyond. It was apparent even before he got there, from the grotesque contortion of the body and the amount of blood seeping through the white ski suit, that the sniper was dead. Booker knelt to pull off the ski mask.

The sniper was the Oriental woman who had met Mhin at the airport.

That definitely settled the question as to which side Mhin Van Thieu was on, Booker thought as he rose to his feet. He climbed back up to the road.

A car heading toward the hotel had stopped because the snowmobile was blocking the left lane. A middle-aged man was driving, with a middle-aged woman alongside of him.

"What's burning down there?" the driver asked Booker, gazing at the black smoke rising from the burning motorcycle.

"Motorcycle went over the drop-off," Booker said. "That's the cycle burning. I just checked the driver. Killed instantly."

"Should we bring him up out of there?" the driver asked, starting to get out of the car.

"No point," Booker said. "Let the cops handle it. You heading for the Squaw Valley Inn?"

The driver nodded. He got back into his car.

"I'm going the other way," Booker said. "Would you mind phoning the cops from the hotel when you get there to tell them about this?"

"Sure," the man said. He looked at the snow-mobile. "You need some help to get that thing off the road?"

"Thanks, but I can manage," Booker told him.

The car pulled around the snowmobile and drove on. Booker pushed the snowmobile off onto the left shoulder of the road, where there was enough snow for traction, jumped onto the seat, and started the engine. Climbing the steep bank, he went over the crest at its top onto fairly level ground, and headed in the opposite direction from the hotel.

If he went back to the hotel, he knew he would be caught up in a police investigation that might hold him up indefinitely. If he told the truth, he figured he would be locked up in protective custody if believed, and held for psychiatric examination if he wasn't believed. The latter seemed more likely, for fear that the CIA, or the FBI, or some other powerful organization was "after" you was a quite common symptom of paranoia.

On the other hand, if he refused to say anything, he probably would be held on suspicion of complicity in Mike Potter's death. It was a no-win situation in which the only intelligent thing to do was disappear.

He decided to find a phone and call Margaret at the hotel.

The slope of the land was steadily downward the farther he got from the hotel. About two miles beyond the point where the motorcycle had gone over the bank, he ran out of snow. Leaving the snowmobile concealed in a clump of underbrush, he continued on foot. Another two miles farther on he came to a service station and diner where there was an outdoor phone booth.

Finding the number of the Squaw Valley Inn, he dropped in a dime and dialed.

18

After the snowmobile with Booker aboard disappeared in pursuit of the sniper, the skiers on the mountaintop emerged from cover and began to descend one at a time to the group below. No one took the jump route, as that might have landed him in the middle of the crowd around Mike Potter's body. The starter was the last one to go down. As he poled himself into the starting box, Margaret realized she was going to be stranded up there all alone.

"Hey," she said. "I haven't any skis. Would you send the tram up for me?"

"Sure, ma'am," he said, and pushed himself off.

It was nearly a half hour before the tram came for her, because the starter had dawdled in the crowd around the body for a time before skiing over to the hotel, and that was another quarter mile farther on. By the time she got down to the hotel, the place was overrun by sheriff's deputies. She tried to sneak through the lobby to her room, but one of the skiers pointed her out to the deputy in charge, and he went over to halt her at the foot of the stairs. He was a burly, pink-faced sergeant in his early thirties.

"Excuse me, ma'am," he said politely. "But may I have a word with you?"

"All right," she agreed.

"I understand that you are here with the man registered as John T. Booker."

"Why do you phrase it that way?" she inquired. "Don't you believe that's his real name?"

"I don't know, ma'am. Is it?"

"Yes."

"May I have your name, ma'am?"

"Margaret Cash."

"May I ask what your relationship with the susp —with Mr. Booker is?"

"He's my lover."

The pink face turned slightly pinker. "I see. How well did you know Mr. Potter, the murder victim?"

"I was introduced to him about two minutes before he was shot."

"By Mr. Booker?"

"Yes."

"What was Mr. Booker's relationship to the murder victim?"

"They were old friends," Margaret said. "They were in Vietnam together. Why are you asking me all these questions, Officer?"

"There has been a suggestion that Mr. Booker may have fingered Potter for the murderer."

Margaret stared at him. "Who was the asshole who made that suggestion?"

The deputy blinked at the word "asshole." He said, "A couple of the people who were up there at the time suggested it. He did make a rather headlong escape immediately after the crime, Miss Cash. And flight tends to be an admission of guilt."

"Your witnesses have their facts twisted. He wasn't running away. He was chasing the murderer."

The burly deputy shook his head. "Witnesses are unanimous that he simply took off across country, not after the killer."

"He was driving a snowmobile, Officer. They need snow to run on. I wondered about that at first, too, but then I figured it out. I think he was circling around to cut off the sniper at the pass, as it were."

"Possibly," the deputy said without any indication of belief. "What does Mr. Booker do for a living, Miss Cash?"

"Well, he's not a Mafia finger man. He's quite respectable. He's a student instructor in political science at the University of California at Los Angeles, working on his Ph.D."

"I never suggested a Mafia association, Miss Cash. But don't you think it strange, if he is entirely innocent, that he hasn't returned by now?"

"No," she said.

He waited for elaboration. When there was none, he started to open his mouth to ask another question but was interrupted by a fellow deputy bringing over a middle-aged couple.

"This is Mr. and Mrs. Perry, Jed," the second deputy said. "They report a motorcycle accident that may be our sniper."

"Oh?" the pink-faced deputy said. "Where was this, folks?"

"About seven miles back on the road from the airport," the man said. "We stopped because this snowmobile was in the middle of the road, and black smoke was rising from something burning down below the road on the opposite side. There's quite a steep drop-off at that point. A man wearing a ski suit came up over the bank and said the smoke was from a burning motorcycle that had plunged over the bank. He said the driver was dead, and asked us to report the accident to the police when we got to the hotel."

The deputy named Jed said to the other one, "Send a team to check that out, Manny. Better send an ambulance too, just in case the victim isn't dead."

Nodding, Manny turned and strode off. Jed turned back to the middle-aged couple.

"What did the man in the ski suit look like?" he asked.

"Tall, quite well built, in his thirties, and had a mustache," Mr. Perry said.

"Quite virile-looking," his wife added.

Her husband looked at her. "What in the hell is virile-looking, Elsie?"

"Like he could—well, you know."

"Make love very thoroughly," Margaret offered helpfully. "Yes, he gives that impression."

"Obviously it was John T. Booker," the pink-faced deputy said to Margaret. Then he turned back to the couple. "Did he give any indication of when he expected to return here?"

"I don't think he expected to," Perry said. "The reason he asked us to report the accident was that he was going the other way. I offered to help him get his snowmobile off the road, but he said he could handle it."

"Thank you, Mr. Perry," the deputy said. "You've been very helpful. You too, Mrs. Perry."

They both told him he was welcome, and moved off toward the registration desk. They heard Perry say to his wife, "Virile-looking, for Christ's sake. You made the officer think you had hot pants for the guy."

"Are you through with me?" Margaret asked the deputy.

"For now," he said. "I'd appreciate it if you didn't leave the hotel without letting me know,

though. And also if you would inform me if Mr.
Booker returns, or if you hear from him."

Giving him a nod that committed her to nothing,
she turned and went up the stairs.

She had a feeling that she would hear from
Booker before long, and that he would ask her to
pick him up somewhere. To be prepared in advance,
she changed out of her ski suit into a skirt and
sweater and packed both suitcases. She carried the
suitcases along the hallway to a door with a lighted
red sign over it reading: FIRE EXIT.

She took the fire stairs downward, pushed
through the fire door, which gave onto the rear
of the hotel, set the suitcases down in the snow,
and held the door open with one foot in it until
she could find a book of matches in her purse. She
set the matchbook in the crack of the door to hold
it open until she returned.

Off in the distance at the ski base she could see
that Mike Potter's body had now been removed.
The only remaining signs of the assassination were
some red stains on the snow and a broken piece of
ski. The onlookers had all returned to the hotel,
and no one was in sight as Margaret carried the
suitcases to the parking lot and locked them in the
trunk of the rented Cobra.

Minutes later she let herself back in by the fire
door, let it swing closed and latch, and returned
to her room.

The phone was ringing as she entered the room.
Picking it up, she said, "Hello?"

"I was about to hang up," Booker's voice said.
"What's happening there?"

"Plenty," Margaret said. "Switchboard operator,
are you on the line?"

When there was no answer, Margaret said, "I
guess there is no one listening, but let's not take

chances. Give me the number you're calling from, and I'll get back to you from a pay phone."

"The hotel doesn't have a pay phone," he told her. "The phone company took it out because nobody used it. We'll have to chance eavesdropping. I'm at a service station and diner about ten or eleven miles from the hotel on the road leading to the airport. It's on the left as you head this way, and it's called Mel's Eatery."

"What an original name," Margaret said.

"Looks like a gourmet place," Booker said. "Pick me up here."

"You'd better wait in some less public place," Margaret advised. "I suspect there's an APB on you."

"For what?"

"There's some suspicion by the deputy sheriff in charge of the investigation that you fingered Mike Potter."

"For Christ's sake, who came up with that brilliant thought?" Booker asked disgustedly.

"Tell you all about it when I see you. Where will that be?"

"Hold it while I look around," Booker said.

Apparently he did his looking from inside the phone booth, because only moments later he said, "The roadside underbrush along here is pretty heavy. I'll wait out of sight just beyond Mel's Eatery. Make sure you aren't tailed."

"Of course," she said. "I shouldn't be long. I anticipated this and already have the suitcases in the trunk of the car."

"Transfer mine to the back seat," he suggested. "I can change out of this ski suit en route."

"Will do," she said. "See you shortly."

She was heading along the hall for the fire exit when the pink-faced deputy named Jed appeared at the top of the stairs from the lobby. She changed direction to head for the stairs.

Stopping her, he said, "The switchboard informs me you just got a phone call, Miss Cash."

"Oh, do you have her listening in to my calls?"

"That's against the law without a court order," he said. "Mind telling me who called you?"

"My mother in L.A. She checks up on me all the time. Particularly when I'm shacked up in some hotel with a man."

"Your mother?" he said without belief. "The switchboard operator said it was a man."

"At first, yes. My father always dials for her, then hands her the phone. Mom's eyesight is nearly gone from years of peering through keyholes. She runs a boardinghouse, you see."

He didn't smile. "You haven't heard from Booker, then?"

"Wouldn't I have informed you if I had, officer? That was your instruction, wasn't it?"

"Yes."

"I was going down for coffee," Margaret said. "Care to join me?"

"Thank you, but I'm afraid I'm too busy just now."

He walked down the stairs with her, but didn't accompany her into the coffee shop. She sat at the counter and had a cup of coffee, then unobtrusively slipped upstairs again. She took the fire stairs down to the back of the hotel, made it to the parking lot without being seen, transferred Booker's suitcase from the car trunk to the back seat, and slipped under the wheel of the rented Cobra.

She drove off the parking lot at low speed, so that the engine sound would be as quiet as possible. In the rear-view mirror she could see that no one had come from the hotel, and that no other car pulled off the lot before she started around the long, sweeping curve a half mile from the hotel. Once she had started around the curve, she was out of sight from the hotel.

19

When Margaret spotted the sign reading MEL'S EATERY, she slowed and examined the underbrush along the left side of the road. About twenty-five yards beyond the service station and diner Booker stepped from the underbrush and flagged her down. When she pulled over on the shoulder, he ran across the road and climbed into the back seat. Margaret immediately pulled away again.

"Jesus," she said. "There were cops all over up there when you called me. Are you all right?"

He pulled the suitcase from the floor up onto the seat beside him and opened it. He began to strip off his ski suit.

"I'm all right," he said. "What gave the cops the idea I fingered Mike?"

"A couple of the skiers up on top with us suggested it. Because you took off across country in the snowmobile. They thought you were running away instead of chasing the sniper."

"And the cops bought that?"

"Not really, I don't think," Margaret said. "When I told the chief investigator you were a graduate student and student instructor at UCLA,

I think it leaned him away from the idea that you were some kind of finger man. But he isn't canceling the idea until he talks to you. I have an idea there will be cops waiting at the airport."

"Then we'll drive out," Booker said. "Look, it's too hard trying to dress in a back seat. Can you pull off somewhere?"

Margaret slowed, spotted a narrow dirt lane off to the right, and pulled into it. She drove along it through the trees and underbrush edging it until they rounded a curve that put them out of sight of the main road.

Getting out of the car, Booker stood alongside of it while he put on his shirt, necktie, and business suit. Margaret got out too, and came around the car to kneel and tie his shoes for him.

When she rose to her feet again, she said, "John, I'm sorry about your friend. Really sorry."

"Yeah," he said. "But there you were, right on the scene again."

Looking at him, she sighed. "Come on, let's talk. Some people came into the hotel and reported to the police that a motorcyclist had been killed by going over a bank. Was it the sniper?"

"Uh-huh."

"You pushed him over the bank?"

"Her."

"Her? Wasn't it Mhin?"

"It was the woman who met him at the airport. What do you want to talk about?"

She took his hand to lead him along a narrow path that led to a clearing through which a narrow stream bubbled. "I told you last night, John," she said, "I'm not an enemy."

They stopped to gaze at the stream, and saw a trout strike a bug on the surface. Margaret looked across the stream at a field of buttercups.

"The cherry blossoms will be coming out around Washington pretty soon," she said musingly.

Becoming conscious that he was gazing at her profile, she turned to look at him. His expression was one of anger and frustration. Moving against him, she put her arms about his neck and looked up into his face with tenderness. He stood unmoving. She pulled his face down to kiss him on the mouth. At first he didn't respond, but then his arms clasped her about the waist and he kissed her hungrily.

Finally he broke the kiss and pushed her away. She moved over to sit on a fallen log, and he crouched on his haunches, gazing into the water.

"Your safety means more to me than any commitments I have," she said. "The hell with everything else. Edgar Harrolds."

He glanced sideways at her. "A childhood sweetheart?"

"The drunk at the cocktail party."

Booker stiffened. "Who is he?"

"Undersecretary of State. A career man at the end of his career. And maybe at the end of his rope."

"Who are you?" Booker asked. "Marilyn Cook of the *Los Angeles Times*, or Margaret Cash of the *Washington Post*?"

"Margaret Cash, but not of the *Washington Post*. I'm not a reporter."

"What are you?"

"Something else. Harrolds worked with Conrad Morgan when Morgan was chief delegate to the Vietnam peace talks. Harrolds hates his guts."

"Conrad Morgan?" Booker said in surprise. "The TV—"

When he didn't finish it, she nodded. "The Senate does more than just question a man who's been nominated for Secretary of State. Before Watergate, it was generally a formality. Nowadays they do a pretty thorough job. They even hire lawyers to investigate.

"I'm sure," he said, coming to his feet. "But what does that—"

"It was really rather funny," she interrupted. "I was invited to the party by the head of the committee. Just a social event. I had barely started working for him."

"You're a lawyer?" Booker said. "An investigator?"

Margaret nodded. "I'd been standing for hours when I noticed this old guy sitting at a table in a corner all alone. He looked pleasantly drunk and harmless, and I was getting tired of being propositioned by half of the upstanding members of Congress, even though most of them looked like they hadn't had anything upstanding in years."

Booker smiled. "That's not one of my problems."

"It certainly isn't," she agreed. "On the contrary. Anyway, I went over and sat with him."

Booker sat on the log next to her. "Is Morgan mixed up in this?"

"Harrolds never went so far as to accuse him outright. But he said a deal had been made with the North Vietnamese chief delegate to give him the Black Tigers in exchange for the release of all other POWs in enemy hands. I don't know who else except our chief delegate could have made such a deal, and Conrad Morgan was our chief delegate."

"I knew we had been sold out," Booker said with feeling. "The son-of-a-bitch. The papers keep saying his approval is assured. How can that be if you told the committee what you just told me?"

"I didn't. You don't survive in Washington by attacking men like Morgan without facts. There is also the ethical factor that a rumor such as that could ruin Morgan's career, and he might be innocent. That's why I didn't want to tell even you. All I told my boss was that I wanted to check out some leads, and he said, 'Go.' "

Booker frowned. "So the committee knows nothing about this?"

"Not yet. That's why we've got to get to Washington."

"We?"

"If you can confront Harrolds with what you went through on that mission, and tell him what's happening now, I think he'll talk. Then we'll have something solid for the committee to use."

"That could take days, and I have a score to settle. Mhin is still alive."

"Forget Mhin. It's more important to me that you stay alive."

She leaned against him, he put his arms around her, and they kissed, briefly but passionately.

"Have you ever considered living in California?" he asked.

She dropped her head onto his shoulder. "I'll miss the cherry blossoms."

He gave her a tender kiss on the forehead, then stood up. "We'd better get moving. They may set up roadblocks when they discover you're missing from the hotel."

They walked back to the car. Booker transferred his suitcase to the trunk and climbed behind the wheel. The lane was too narrow to turn around in, so he had to back out to the main road.

As they started on, Margaret said, "What can they do to you for failure to return a rented car? Charge you with auto theft?"

"You can turn these in anywhere," Booker said. "I'll turn it in when I drop you at the airport."

"I wasn't thinking about this car, but the one I left in San Diego," she said. "What do you mean, drop me? You really aren't going to Washington with me?"

"I have to track down Mhin, honey."

"In L.A.? Seems to me you'd have more luck hunting around here."

"Hit men don't hang around once a job is pulled," Booker said. "By now he's scrammed the hell out of this area. I plan to get Murray Saunders' help to track him down. Murray has resources I couldn't match."

"If that's the way it has to be," she said with a sigh. "Okay, I'll fly to Washington alone."

They rounded a curve and suddenly were confronted by two cars parked sideways across the road, blocking both lanes. They were not sheriff's cars, but as Booker slowed, two men in the uniforms of sheriff's deputies stepped from the underbrush on the left side of the road with leveled pistols.

Booker came to a complete stop and pulled over on the shoulder. He examined the two uniformed men ruefully as they approached. One was tall and lean and almost albino, with platinum blond hair and a pale, narrow face. The other was a burly 220-pounder with a square head and cold blue eyes.

"Looks like we're going to be delayed after all," Booker said to Margaret in a resigned tone.

"Get out of the car, please," the tall, pale man said.

Booker and Margaret got out of opposite sides of the car. The burly man moved around onto the shoulder to cover Margaret, while the pale man kept his gun trained on Booker.

"You can put that away," Booker said. "We're not resisting."

Instead the man cocked the gun. As Booker suddenly realized that a man in a police uniform isn't necessarily a real cop, the man's trigger finger began to whiten. Instinctively Booker's right foot swung upward to kick the gun into an upward arc. It went off, but the slug whistled a foot over Booker's head. The kick didn't dislodge the gun from the man's grip, though, because of necessity it had been too hurried. The gun started to come down again.

This time Booker planted the inner side of his foot beneath the man's chin, raising him a couple of inches into the air before he collapsed on his back, unconscious.

Booker dived into the underbrush before the uniformed man on the other side of the car could get around it. A shot sounded and a slug plunked into the trunk of the tree he was scrambling behind. He ran on, keeping the tree between himself and the cars until he reached the safety of an even thicker tree. Dropping prone behind it, he glanced around the tree trunk.

The burly man was peering his way, but he quickly gave up the idea of pursuit through all that underbrush and trees. Probably part of the reason was eagerness to get out of there before any real deputies came along.

Picking up his unconscious partner's dropped gun, the burly man shoved it under his belt. Then he made Margaret turn around and handcuffed her wrists behind her. He made her sit in the front seat of the car blocking the left lane, and dragged his unconscious partner over and heaved him onto the floor of the back seat.

After peering toward Booker again, the man pulled the other car off the road onto the shoulder, parking it in front of the rented Cobra, then reached into the Cobra to remove the keys. He peered in Booker's direction again, then took out a small card, wrote something on it with a pen, and tossed it onto the car's front seat.

Climbing behind the wheel of the car containing Margaret and his unconscious partner, the burly man drove off in the direction of the Squaw Valley Inn.

20

As soon as the car was out of sight, Booker ran across the road and picked up the card the burly man had tossed onto the front seat of the Cobra. It was a plain business card reading *Paul Gibbons* and giving a San Francisco post office box and telephone number. There was no indication of what the man's business was.

Murray Saunders carried similar cards. They were standard in the CIA.

On the back of the card had been written: *Phone local 642–1041 in one hour.*

Booker checked the car parked in front of the Cobra, not really expecting to find a key in the ignition, but hoping. There wasn't one.

He knew there were no tools in the trunk of the rented Cobra that he could use to jump the ignition, but there might be in the other car. He opened the locked trunk by the simple process of leaping into the air and giving it a powerful two-footed kick. As he landed on his hands and flipped himself erect, the trunk lid popped open.

There were enough tools in the trunk to serve his purpose. With a pair of pliers he snipped off a length of the exposed taillight wire and used it to jump the ignition of the Cobra. Then he had to disassemble the steering column in order to unlock the steering wheel, and put it back together again. By the time he finished and had the Cobra in running order, the other car had been gone for a half hour. He made no attempt to chase after it.

Returning to Mel's Eatery, Booker peered inside, saw no cops, and ventured in. He got a couple of dollars change from the proprietor and went out to the outdoor phone booth.

When he gave the operator Murray Saunders' number in Los Angeles, she told him to drop a dollar thirty cents for three minutes. Saunders answered in the middle of the first ring.

"You must have been sitting on the phone," Booker said.

"Got the jitters," the CIA agent said. "Been worried about you."

"I'm the only one left, Murray. They got Gordie Jones and Joe Walker yesterday, Mike Potter today."

"Jesus," Saunders said. "Where are you?"

"Squaw Valley. Do you know a Paul Gibbons?"

"Sure. He's in charge of the San Francisco office."

"And a tall, thin, pale man, almost an albino, who works with him?"

"Tom Fade," Saunders said. "Christ, he isn't on you, is he?"

"Both of them."

"Run, John. Run like hell. Tom Fade is the Company's most efficient hit man. You won't stand a chance against him. He's not only deadly, he's a master con artist. He'll charm you into standing still while he puts a bullet in your brain."

"He tried it once. All it got him was a sore jaw."

"You tangled and came out on top? Quit while you're ahead, John. Run."

"He's got Margaret Cash, Murray."

After a period of silence, Saunders said, "That's the same as Marilyn Cook?"

"Uh-huh."

"So?"

"She's become rather special to me."

"Oh. That complicates things. All I can do is give you advice. Fade can charm the whiskers off a tiger. He'll use the girl to talk you into walking into a trap. If you're gullible, you'll believe him and walk into it. Don't believe one fucking thing he says. He's out to kill you."

"Okay, Murray, thanks for the advice."

"You're welcome. Good luck, John. You're going to need it."

Hanging up, Booker looked at his watch. It was almost eleven, which meant he still had fifteen minutes before he was supposed to call the phone number on the card. He went back into Mel's Eatery and killed it dawdling over a cup of bitter coffee.

At 11:15 he returned to the booth and dialed 642–1041. Booker recognized the voice that answered as that of the tall, pale man who had attempted to shoot him.

When the man said, "Hello," Booker said, "Apparently you recovered."

"Not completely," Tom Fade said in a slightly slurred voice. "You kick hard, Mr. Booker."

"What do you want?" Booker asked.

"My partner and I would like to meet with you for a little conference."

"You mean walk into a trap, so you can gun me down?" Booker said. "No thanks."

"You have the wrong idea, Mr. Booker. We simply want to talk to you, not kill you."

"Then why didn't you talk before, instead of trying to shoot me without warning?"

"You thought I was going to shoot you?" Fade said, aghast at the idea.

"Weren't you?"

"Of course not. I was merely going to order you to turn around and then put handcuffs on you, but you suddenly started using your feet. The only reason I was going to handcuff you was that we feared you would object to going off with us, and we really have to have this talk. We want to stop all this senseless killing. Mhin Van Thieu apparently has gone nuts."

The man's tone was so convincing that Booker might have believed him if it hadn't been for Murray Saunders' advice, and Booker's memory of that whitening trigger finger just before he kicked Fade's gun barrel upward. There was no doubt in his mind that the pale man had intended to kill him at the roadblock. There was no doubt in his mind that the "conference" was planned to complete the job. But there would be no advantage in letting the man know that Booker considered him a liar.

"Is Margaret all right?" he asked.

"Of course, Mr. Booker. We mean her no harm. We simply took her off because we thought that might give you more inducement to call. We are not holding her safety over your head to force you to cooperate, however, because we are not kidnappers. We hope to convince you of the advantage of meeting with us purely through reason."

"Then you'll release her even if I don't show?"

Fade said smoothly, "Well, it is extremely important to us that we meet with you. And it would be more convenient for all concerned if you picked her up here at the same time you came for the conference. Don't you agree?"

"Do I have a choice? Where is here?"

"We have a rented cabin about five miles beyond the Squaw Valley Inn. Follow the same road that takes you from the airport to the Inn until you see a sign for Bolero Canyon Road going off to the right. Follow Bolero Canyon to its very end. You can't miss it, because its the only house on the road."

"All right," Booker said. "I'll come out to talk to you. One stipulation, though. I want to talk to Margaret now."

"Of course," Fade said courteously. "One moment."

After a short wait, Margaret's voice said, "John?"

"Yes, honey. Are you all right?"

"Yes. John, these men say they're on our side, that they want to end the killing. They say Mhin has been doing this on his own, and they think he's crazy. They sound convincing, but I don't know. What do you think?"

"They sound convincing to me too," he lied. "It can't hurt to listen to what they have to say. I'll see you shortly. Meantime let me talk to that blond guy again."

When Tom Fade came back on the phone, Booker asked, "When do you want me out there?"

"Within the next hour, if that's convenient."

"Okay," Booker said. "See you within the hour."

Hanging up, he left the booth and climbed into the Cobra. He headed for the airport.

He had only a tentative plan, because no detailed plan was possible until he saw the lay of the land. From the pale man's description, it had sounded as though the cabin was at the end of a box canyon, which allowed only a frontal approach in an automobile. It might be impossible to approach from any other way regardless of how he arrived, but Booker intended to have the necessary equipment with him in case there was some possibility.

He assumed that police would be posted at the airport to watch for him, but they would be watching the reservation desks and the boarding gates, not the shops. He spotted no uniforms in the shopping area.

In a sporting goods store he bought a pair of skis and poles. He got back to the car without incident and stowed the skis in it, resting them on the back window ledge and the backrest of the front seat on the passenger side.

Driving back to where he had abandoned the snowmobile, he loaded the skis and poles onto it, then changed into his ski suit. He had to push the snowmobile a short distance to snow, but then he mounted the seat, started the engine, and took off.

He traveled parallel to the road and as close to it as the trees and underbrush edging it would allow. But when he neared the Squaw Valley Inn, he skirted widely around it to come back to the road a mile beyond it. Four miles after that he spotted the crossroads sign for Bolero Canyon Road.

He drove near enough to see that it was a canyon road with steep banks on both sides. It had to be a box canyon, because a low mountain rose only a couple of hundred yards back from the main road.

He didn't want to drive close enough to the canyon edge to see the cabin nestled at the end of the road, because that would have made him visible from it also. Instead he made a wide circle and came up behind it, halfway up the mountainside.

He couldn't see the cabin from that vantage point either, because it was below a steep drop-off. He could see the road coming in from the main road, though. It was narrow, and only a car-width lane down its center had been plowed in the snow.

Cutting the idling engine of the snowmobile, Booker got off and tied on his skis. The way down to the drop-off was sheer, but he held down his speed by zigzagging back and forth. Fifty feet from the edge of the drop-off, the cabin came into view. He halted to examine it. It was a low, one-story building with a peaked roof whose center beam ran from front to rear. The roof was covered with at least six inches of snow.

Booker pointed his skis forward and poled himself toward the edge of the drop-off with powerful thrusts that had him moving at high speed by the time he reached it. He soared over the edge in a crouch and made a perfect landing on the cabin roof fifty feet below, one ski on either side of the peak. He skidded to a halt only inches from the front end of the roof.

If his landing had been heard, it must have been dismissed as the sound of thawing snow sliding off the roof, because there was no reaction from below. Untying his skis, Booker ran across the roof peak to the rear of the cabin and jumped down into a soft snowbank against the cliffside behind the building.

Floundering out of the snowbank, Booker moved to the back door and tried it. The door was locked. He made a leap through the air and lashed out at it with both feet. The door burst inward off its hinges.

Landing on his hands and flipping himself back onto his feet, Booker stepped into a kitchen just as the burly Paul Gibbons ran into it with a leveled pistol. Booker threw himself in a feet-first slide at the man's legs just as the gun went off.

The bullet winged harmlessly over the horizontal

Booker and out the door as Booker's feet collided with the burly man's knees. With a squeal of pain the man pitched forward. Booker was up and after him before Gibbons stopped sliding along the floor on his face. Gripping both ankles, Booker swung the man in an arc that ended with his head smashing against the sink with the sound of a burst pumpkin.

Releasing his grip on the dead man's ankles, Booker scooped up his dropped gun and charged through the kitchen door into the front room. He skidded to a halt when he saw the pale-faced Tom Fade, his left arm circling Margaret's neck from behind and his pistol to her head.

"Just hold it right there," Fade said. "Drop the gun or I'll blow her brains out."

Booker tilted up his gun and fired from the hip. A red-ringed hole appeared in the pale man's forehead and he fell over backward, dragging Margaret with him.

"You could have killed me instead," she whispered as Booker helped her to her feet.

"No way," he said. "I'm a snapshot expert. Which just goes to show you that you should know your opponent's talents before you deliver an ultimatum."

Booker went into the kitchen and recovered the keys for the Cobra from the pocket of the dead man there. Then, as an afterthought, he pressed the gun that had killed Tom Fade into the dead man's hand.

Margaret, who had followed after him, asked, "Why are you doing that?"

"Just to give the cops something to puzzle out," he said. "Call it my pixie sense of humor."

Margaret shivered. "It's cold in here with that door off its hinges."

"Then let's get out," Booker suggested. "It's warm where I left the Cobra parked."

He left the skis on the roof, and left Mike Potter's snowmobile parked on the mountainside in back of the cabin. They took the CIA men's car, and abandoned it where Booker had left the rented Cobra. As Booker had said, it was considerably warmer there, because it was a couple of thousand feet lower.

Booker turned off into the same narrow lane that Margaret had previously driven into so that he could change from his ski suit back into his business suit. When they started on again, Margaret asked where they were going.

"Nearest airport of any size is San Francisco," Booker said. "Only logical place to go."

21

From CIA headquarters in San Francisco Mhin Van Thieu dialed station-to-station number 642–1041 at Squaw Valley. He was all alone in the office.

A male voice he didn't recognize said, "Hello?"

"Paul Gibbons, please," Mhin said.

"He can't come to the phone just now. May I take a message?"

"Who are you?" Mhin asked.

"Just a friend. Who are you?"

Ignoring the counter-question, Mhin said, "Let me speak to Tom Fade."

"He's tied up too at the moment."

He was talking to a cop, Mhin realized. He hung

up. Immediately he dialed another number, this time in Washington, D.C.

When a female voice answered, he said, "This is Mhin Van Thieu, Code Three-seven-two. I need some information fast."

"Go ahead, Three-seven-two."

"Paul Gibbons and Tom Fade of the San Francisco office have a rented mountain cabin on Bolero Canyon Road at Squaw Valley. I just phoned there, and a cop answered. Said neither one could come to the phone. Will you make an official inquiry and get back to me at the San Francisco office?"

"Will do, Three-seven-two."

The return call came thirty minutes later. When Mhin answered, the female voice said, "Three-seven two?"

"Yes," Mhin said.

"Agents Gibbons and Fade are both dead, apparently murdered. The sheriff's office at Squaw Valley says a gun gripped in Gibbons' hand killed Fade, then someone else bashed out Gibbons' brains. The back door of the cabin was off its hinges, as though bashed in by something like a battering ram. Also a pair of skis and ski poles were found on the roof, and there was an abandoned snowmobile on the mountainside behind the cabin."

"Thanks," Mhin said. "That answers all my questions."

Hanging up, he brooded over this information. There was no doubt in his mind that John Booker was responsible for what had happened at the mountain cabin, because it had all the earmarks of the ex-commander of the Black Tigers. Now what would be Booker's next move?

He would avoid the airport at Squaw Valley, Mhin surmised, because he would be afraid the police might be covering it. Which meant he would have to drive out. And logically he would head for San Francisco, because that was the nearest major airport. It seemed unlikely he would drive all the way to Los Angeles.

Mhin put on a simple disguise consisting of a Vandyke beard and sunglasses. Then, from a storage cabinet, he took some gelignite, a fuse, and a timing device. Gingerly packing them into a small leather carrying case, he carried the case down to the office building parking lot and stowed it in the trunk of the blue Celica.

He drove to the San Francisco Airport. Leaving the car in the parking lot, he entered the main terminal building.

It was about 6:00 P.M. when he got there. By eight he was beginning to suspect he had guessed Booker's plans wrong. He was about ready to give up when he saw Booker and Margaret Cash enter the building. Booker was carrying two suitcases.

The couple went over to study the flight schedule board, then went up to a ticket counter. Mhin drifted over to a flight insurance machine only a few feet from the ticket counter, dropped some coins and, with his back to Booker and Margaret, began to fill out the form that was spewed from the machine.

Margaret asked the girl behind the counter, "Is there space for one on Flight Three-twenty-two to Washington?"

The girl consulted a list. "Yes, ma'am. Round trip or one way?"

"Round trip," Booker said. "Back to L.A. instead of here, though." He smiled at Margaret. "You'll be needing it."

Also smiling, Margaret said to the girl, "You heard the man. Sounds like a commitment, doesn't it?"

Laughing, the reservation clerk began to write up the ticket.

Booker said, "Make mine one-way to L.A., please, on Flight Eighteen."

Mhin walked away, circled around, and went over to look at the flight schedule board. Flight Three-twenty-two to Washington left in one hour. Flight Eighteen to Los Angeles left in an hour and a half. The former's boarding gate was ten, the latter's, four.

Mhin went out to the parking lot, got the leather carrying case from the trunk of the Celica, carried it back to the terminal and stored it in a coin locker near the hallway running to Gate Ten.

Then he went hunting for airport police.

He spotted and rejected three-before he finally located one of about his size and build. The man was standing next to a coffee machine, sipping coffee from a plastic cup.

Approaching him, Mhin said, "I'm Detective Sergeant Chen of Burglary Division. I just caught two juveniles breaking into a car in the parking lot. I have one handcuffed to the door of the car, but the other ran away. I'd like to turn the one over to the custody of the airport police while I try to track down the other."

"Sure, Sergeant," the man said.

Gulping the rest of his coffee, he dropped the plastic cup in a nearby trash can and followed Mhin to the parking lot.

Mhin led the way over to the Celica in the center of the lot, his gaze flicking around in all directions en route to check for possible witnesses. There were none close enough to make out what was going to happen.

Then they reached the Celica, Mhin said in a surprised voice, "Hey, he's gone." Then he pointed behind the uniformed man and said, "There he is!"

When the officer spun around, Mhin smashed the hard edge of his right palm alongside the man's neck from behind. The policeman dropped without a sound.

Quickly Mhin stripped off the unconscious man's gunbelt and uniform. Unlocking the trunk, he heaved the limp body inside, pushing the man's knees up to his chest in order to make him fit. Stripping off his own outer clothing, he tossed it into the trunk and donned the police uniform.

While it wasn't unusual for a plainclothesman to be bearded, few men in uniform were, and Mhin had spotted none among the airport police. So as not to attract undue attention, he removed his false Vandyke beard and dropped it into the trunk too. He kept on his sunglasses, though. He headed back for the terminal.

Getting his leather carrying case from the coin locker, he unlocked and opened it, holding it so that no one nearby could see its contents. After setting the timing device for five minutes after the takeoff time of Flight 322, he closed and locked it again. He carried it over to Gate Ten.

"Flight Three-twenty-two landed yet?" he asked the ticket taker.

"Just," the man said. He examined the leather case curiously.

"Special high priority cargo for the personal custody of the pilot," Mhin explained.

He went out the gate and over to the waiting C–47. A ground crew was fueling the plane, and a baggage crew was loading baggage.

He climbed the mobile stairway and was met at the top by a stewardess.

"Special delivery from the commander of the airport police to the commander of the airport police in Washington," he said, handing her the leather case. "Will you take care of it?"

"Sure, Sergeant," she said.

Turning, he went back down the stairs. The stewardess stowed the case in the luggage compartment at the front of the plane.

Although they had plenty of time, Booker and Margaret had been too busy discussing their future together to think of eating dinner. They had simply sat in the waiting room, holding hands and talking.

When the loudspeaker announced that passengers were now boarding Flight 322 at Gate Ten, Booker belatedly realized that they hadn't eaten.

"I should have bought you dinner," he said contritely as he rose to his feet. "I doubt that you'll be able to get anything on the plane this late."

Smiling at him as she also rose, she said, "I can live on love that far."

"How about a farewell cup of coffee anyway?" Booker suggested, indicating a nearby vending machine.

"Why not?" she said. "We can drink it en route to the gate."

Booker dropped coins and got two cups of coffee in plastic cups. They moved toward the gate slowly, sipping the coffee on the way.

"Everything's happening so fast," she said wistfully. "I wish I didn't have to leave so soon."

"We'll make up for it," he assured her.

They reached the line formed at the boarding gate. There was a long enough line so that they finished their coffee by the time Margaret reached the ticket taker. Booker took her empty cup from her.

"I'll do my damnedest to get them to delay the confirmation," Margaret said. "But I'll need you there to stop it, if Harrolds will talk."

"I'll be there day after tomorrow," Booker said.

Giving him a quick kiss of good-bye, she went through the turnstile, then turned.

"Gonna wave good-bye?" she asked.

"I have to turn in the rental car."

She laughed. "Oh, God, I still have one with the meter running in San Diego."

"The committee will love you," Booker said. "They can ask for a bigger car-rental budget next year. Don't worry about us taxpayers."

He blew her a kiss, laughing, and turned away. She gazed after him for a moment, then turned and ran for the plane.

22

In the baggage room several passengers from a just-landed jet were waiting for their luggage to come down the chute. Redcaps were helping some people collect their bags, while others grabbed their own.

Through a chain-link fence at the rear of the baggage area Mhin Van Thieu watched the C–47 Margaret Cash was aboard begin to roar down the field for takeoff. He was still in the uniform of an airport cop.

At that moment Booker was walking out the main door of the terminal building toward the parking lot across the road. He could hear Margaret's plane taking off on the other side of the terminal building. When he got across the street, he paused before entering the lot and turned to watch the plane rise above the building. He had a wide smile on his face.

The smile was wiped out by a deafening explosion. He stared in disbelief as the plane was engulfed in a huge ball of flame.

"My God, Margaret!" he shouted as he ran back toward the terminal building at full speed. "Margaret!"

Inside the building he raced toward the area of closest access to the field, the baggage room. The people in there were yelling and shouting and pointing toward the field, where the crashed plane was now obscured by a dense cloud of black smoke. Most were crowding to the fence for a better view, but one man in the uniform of an airport policeman was rapidly walking away.

He had taken only two or three steps when he was slammed into by the running Booker. Both staggered backward.

"Excuse me, sir," Mhin started to say, then there was instant and simultaneous recognition.

"Mhin!" Booker said, enraged with sudden realization that he was face-to-face with the man who had killed Margaret. "You bastard!"

Another, smaller, explosion and a flash of flame came from the smoke-shrouded wreckage, causing Booker to throw an agonized glance that way. Mhin instantly took advantage of it by flying at Booker with a karate kick. At the last instant Booker sensed it coming and rolled with the kick, so that it failed to put him out of action, although it did knock him down.

Instantly he was up again and launched a return kick at Mhin. The Oriental dodged, then dived in headfirst to drive his head into Booker's stomach, again knocking him down, but this time also landing prone himself.

Both bounced erect. Belatedly Mhin thought of the policeman's gun strapped to his waist and jerked it from its holster. An expertly placed kick sent it flying from his grip to arc over the chain-link fence and come down on the concrete on the other side.

The fight was then on in earnest, as both karate experts exercised their lethal skills. The dueling pair knocked each other over luggage, knocked down spectators who got too close, rolled over counters and baggage carts, and knocked over a couple of pet carriers that burst open, releasing a dog from one and a cat from the other. The cat took off in hissing flight as the dog yapped after it.

There were no security police around to interrupt the fight, because the exploding plane had drawn them all out onto the field.

Booker was gradually getting the upper hand when he stumbled backward over a fat woman bystander and landed on an empty baggage cart. Mhin gave the cart a mighty shove that rolled it away at high speed, and made a dash for the front door of the terminal.

As Booker rolled off of the speeding cart, two male bystanders decided to come to the assistance of what they thought was an airport policeman, and jumped on him from either side. All that got them was a pair of headaches when he banged their heads together, but it delayed him enough for Mhin to reach his Celica in the parking lot by the time Booker ran through the entry gate to the lot.

The Celica's engine started, the compact backed, then gunned toward Booker as the latter raced toward it. As the car and the running man closed, the car rapidly accelerating and Booker running at

it at full speed, Booker made a tremendous leap
and flew feet first at the Celica's windshield. With a
shattering crash his feet burst right through the
windshield and slammed into the driver's face.

As the car veered out of control, Booker rolled
from the hood onto the concrete. He sat on the
ground for a moment as the compact crashed into
a light pole and its engine died.

Leaping to his feet, Booker ran over to the car
and jerked open the door on the driver's side.
Mhin's body rolled out onto the concrete, his
broken neck twisted at an impossible angle.

After gazing down at the body for a moment,
Booker shifted his gaze toward the terminal building. Heavy black smoke was still rising from
beyond the building, and people could still be
heard shouting. The sirens of fire engines and am-
bulances sounded.

Booker became conscious of a knocking sound
coming from inside the Celica's trunk. Getting the
keys from the ignition, he unlocked and opened
the trunk. A man in his underwear was uncomfort-
ably folded up inside the small trunk.

"I guess you must be the cop he got the uniform
from," Booker said as he helped the man out.

Stiffly straightening up, but holding his wry neck
at a painful angle, the man gazed at the dead Mhin.
"Yes," he said. "Who are you?"

Booker didn't answer because he was running
for his rented Cobra. There was nothing he could
do for Margaret now, and all that waiting around
would get him would be the delay of trying to
explain to the police what had happened. Slipping
behind the wheel, he drove to the exit, paid his
parking fee, and drove off the lot.

The policeman was too busy getting his uniform

off the dead man and back onto himself to call a challenge after Booker.

It was 450 miles from San Francisco to Los Angeles, but Booker decided to drive it. He knew that if he tried to keep his flight reservation, some bystander was almost sure to recognize him from the fight with Mhin and point him out to airport police. Besides, grief for Margaret made it impossible for him to submit to anything as passive as an airplane ride. He needed a high-speed drive to quell his grief and rage.

He wished he was driving the Porsche instead of the Cobra because he could have made the trip in three-fourths of the time. He still made pretty good time, though. It was about 9:30 P.M. when he left the airport. Stopping only for gasoline, he barreled the whole distance at seventy-five to eighty-five miles an hour, and reached his apartment in West Los Angeles at 3:30 in the morning.

He fell into bed exhausted, almost instantly dropped asleep, but had nightmares about Margaret in the burning plane all during the four hours he was able to sleep. He popped awake at 7:30 A.M., knowing that sleep was finished for him until he could again drive himself to exhaustion.

By the time he had showered, shaved, dressed, and made himself a cup of instant coffee, it was 8:00 A.M.. Carrying the coffee over to the phone, he dialed Murray Saunders' home number.

The CIA agent answered with a sleepy, "Hello?"

"I have to see you right away," Booker said.

"Jesus, you survived," Saunders said. "You woke me up. I was working with the computer until three in the morning."

"I was awake until three-thirty," Booker told him. "How soon can you get to your office?"

"Forty-five minutes," Saunders said. "I want to

talk to you, too. According to the computer, Paul Gibbons, Tom Fade, and a CIA hit woman named Ai-ling Jui-kiuo are dead. You responsible?"

"Your computer isn't up to date," Booker told him. "You can add the hit man who killed Joe Walker down in Mexico, and Mhin Van Thieu."

"Jesus," Saunders said. "You sure evened the score. Five Black Tigers and five of our guys. When did you cut down Mhin?"

"Last night at the San Francisco Airport, right after he blew up the plane with Margaret aboard."

"He was responsible for that?" Saunders asked in a surprised voice. "I heard about it on the air. Margaret was on that flight?"

"I'm trying not to think about it," Booker said bitterly. "See you in forty-five minutes."

Booker was waiting at the office on Figueroa Street when Murray Saunders got there. The black man led the way into his private office and locked the door behind them. Seating himself behind his desk, he lit a cigar.

"Sorry about your girl friend, John," he said with sympathy.

"She was a little more than just a girl friend," Booker said with bitterness, restlessly pacing up and down. "We had some future plans." Then he made a dismissing gesture. "She's gone, and grieving isn't going to bring her back. I prefer to concentrate on getting the son-of-a-bitch responsible for her death."

"Do you know who that is?"

"Sure. Conrad Morgan."

Saunders took the cigar from his mouth to stare at Booker unbelievingly. "The Secretary of State Designate?" he asked in a slightly high voice.

"You know any other Conrad Morgans in a

position to plant false information in your computer bank?" Booker inquired sourly.

"Jesus, are you sure?"

"Not absolutely," Booker admitted. "But my information came from Margaret, and she was in a pretty good position to know. She wasn't a reporter, Murray. And her real name was Margaret Cash."

"What was she?" the black man asked.

"A lawyer investigator for the Senate committee holding hearings on Morgan."

"I'll be damned," Saunders said. "What did she have on Morgan?"

"Only suspicion, but pretty well substantiated suspicion. An old man named Edgar Harrolds, one of the Undersecretaries of State, got drunk at a Washington cocktail party and sounded off to her."

"Edgar Harrolds? Hell, I know him. He was Morgan's aide when Morgan was chief delegate to the Vietnam Peace Talks."

Nodding, Booker said, "That's the man. He claimed somebody made a deal with the chief delegate of the North Vietnamese to give him the Black Tigers in exchange for the safe return of all other POWs."

A strange expression appeared on Saunders' face. "That was it," he said softly. "General Kuong Yin never threatened to kill those hundred-and-fifty CIA people he had prisoner. He just wanted the Black Tigers. And that son-of-a-bitch Morgan agreed to give you guys to him."

"Harrolds never specifically named Conrad Morgan," Booker said. "But Margaret figured it had to be him, because nobody else was in a position to make such a deal."

"Of course it was him," Saunders said, clapping himself on the side of the head. "Jesus Christ, I should have put it together in Saigon. It was a setup all the way."

Booker said, "I was planning to meet Margaret in Washington tomorrow. She thought if I talked to Harrolds and told him what has been going on, he might open up and give us the proof we need."

"Then Washington ought to be our next stop," Saunders said.

"You'll come along?" Booker said in surprise. "I thought you wanted to avoid direct involvement."

"That was before I realized a murdering bastard could become our next Secretary of State if I just sit on my duff." The black man pulled his desk phone in front of him. "Shall I get reservations on the flight to Washington?"

"The sooner the better," Booker said. "There's still something I don't understand about this, though, Murray."

"What?"

"Why Morgan suddenly decided to have the Black Tigers who survived that mission killed off."

"Maybe he found out that Harrolds was about to crack."

"Then why didn't he just arrange an 'accident' for Harrolds?"

"Five'll get you ten there's a damn good reason he didn't."

Booker nodded agreement. "Let's go find out."

"What I was planning to do when you sidetracked me," Saunders said.

Picking up the phone, he dialed a number.

23

Their plane touched down at the airport in Washington at 3:00 P.M. They took a taxi into town. Murray Saunders gave the driver the address of an apartment building on Pennsylvania Avenue.

It was a rather old but well-kept-up building of six stories. In a recessed area just outside the front entrance there were several banks of mailboxes. Only about half had name cards on them. The name Edgar Harrolds was not among those that had cards.

"Awful lot of vacant apartments," Booker commented.

"There aren't any vacant apartments in Washington," Saunders informed him. "Just a lot of vacant people who don't want the general public to know where they live. We'll have to get the manager or somebody to show us to Harrolds' apartment."

They went in to a large lobby, quaintly furnished with mid-Victorian furniture and a huge, expensive Oriental rug. Just inside the door was a counter with a plump, thirtyish security guard in a tan uniform behind it.

"Ah," Saunders said to Booker. "We won't have to disturb the manager after all." To the security guard he said, "Ed Harrolds' apartment, please."

"May I have your names?" the guard asked.

"We want to surprise him," Saunders said.

"We don't allow our tenants to be surprised."

Saunders produced an excellently forged ID identifying him as an FBI agent and showed it to the man.

After politely examining it, the guard said, "You

could be Mr. J. Edgar Hoover, and I still couldn't let you go upstairs without first phoning. Mr. Harrolds has specifically requested that no one be allowed to visit him without his personal authorization."

Booker said, "It's not likely he could be Mr. Hoover, even if he wanted to. Not only is he the wrong color, but Mr. Hoover's dead."

"I'm sure you get my meaning," the guard said with a touch of condescension.

"Yes, we do," Saunders said. "Now we want you to be sure to get ours." He aimed a thumb at Booker. "My friend here is very cranky. In fact, I'd say he's on the very edge of anger. And in just about five seconds I'm going to ask him to kick your teeth in if you don't walk over to that bank of elevators and show us the way to Mr. Harrolds' apartment."

After studying Booker's muscular frame, an apprehensive look formed on the guard's face. Without another word he came out from behind the counter and headed for the bank of elevators.

"They must be his own teeth," Booker said as he and Saunders followed.

The guard punched the button for the third floor. As they started up, he said in a slightly shaking voice, "Was that a real identification card? I mean, you aren't robbers, are you? Or kidnappers? The reason I ask is that Mr. Harrolds has been acting as though he were afraid someone is after him. He almost never comes out of his apartment anymore."

Booker and Saunders merely gazed at him curiously. The elevator door opened at the third floor, they all got out, then the guard turned to face them.

In a rather pompous tone he began a lecture. "No,

I don't think so. This is political, isn't it? Perhaps you gentlemen remember the last time a Washington apartment was broken into for political reasons. Just think about it, gentlemen. It altered the course of history."

Saunders said, "My friend here is going to alter the course of your nose if you don't take us to the door."

Eyeing Booker, the guard said, "Well, of course, when you put it in that perspective—"

Then he jumped when Booker said, "Now!"

Turning, he led them along the hallway and around a corner, stopping before a door numbered 333 with an empty nameplate below the numbers.

Saunders said to Booker, "Question is, shall we ring the buzzer, shall we open it with my tools, or shall I let you kick it in?" He turned to the guard. "What do you think?"

"I would prefer you ring the buzzer."

"I thought you would," Booker said.

Saunders pressed the doorbell. Inside they could hear a buzzer sounding.

"So far, so good," Saunders said to the security guard.

From the other side of the door a cautious male voice said, "Yes?"

Saunders whispered to the guard, "Tell him it's you."

Also whispering, the guard said, "It's me, Mr. Harrolds."

"Who?" the voice behind the door asked.

Saunders whispered, "Be a little more specific. Or louder, maybe."

"Albert," the guard said in his normal voice.

Saunders made an up gesture with his palms, a signal for Albert to speak even louder.

"The guard from the lobby," Albert nearly shouted.

"What do you want?" Harrolds asked through the door.

Saunders whispered to the guard, "Package."

"Package," the guard said loudly.

At the sound of an interior lock turning, Booker and Saunders stepped to either side of the door. The door opened a few inches, but was still on a chain latch.

Saunders whispered across to Booker, "I think we'll need some kicking after all."

"You've got it," Booker said as he kicked the door open, breaking the burglar chain.

The door banged into Edgar Harrolds, driving him backward and sloshing the glass of whiskey in his hand all over his shirt front.

The man was even more stooped and wrinkled than the last time Saunders had seen him in Paris. At only about sixty-five he was an old man. He was in neatly pressed suit pants, a blue button-down Oxford shirt, and bright red suspenders. He looked about three-quarters drunk.

The kicked-in door put a momentary look of fear on his face, but when he saw Saunders, it was replaced by one of mere resignation.

"The violence wouldn't have been necessary if you had announced your name, Mr. Saunders," he said. Then, to the guard, "It's all right, Albert."

Saunders motioned Booker to go into the apartment, followed after him, then turned to say to the security guard, "You've been very civilized. Thank you."

Shrugging, Albert moved away toward the elevators. Saunders closed the door. Booker and Saunders glanced around the front room of the apartment. It was neat and clean and well-furnished, but it had the austere air of bachelorhood about it, the room of one used to living alone.

"Good afternoon, Mr. Harrolds," Saunders said. "Sorry we spilled your drink."

Harrolds glanced down at his soaked shirt front then over at the broken chain on the door. "My vengeance is swift, saith the Lord. I expected it to be swift, and very violent. I have not been disappointed. Since the day you walked out of my life in that Paris hotel room, Mr. Saunders, I've been wondering if you might not return. The fact that you're here is a testimony to your powers of survival."

Saunders said, "I'm afraid the test is not over yet. I'd like you to meet John Booker."

Harrolds looked at Booker without surprise, but with considerable interest. He didn't offer his hand. With a sardonic quirk of a smile on his face he said, "Major Booker, the shepherd of the betrayed flock."

"That's what we're here to talk about," Booker said.

Nodding, Harrolds tossed off the few drops of whiskey remaining in his glass, crossed the room to a small server loaded with liquor bottles, and poured himself another. "Would either of you like a drink?" he asked with his back to them.

"It's a little early for me," Saunders said. Booker merely said, "No."

Turning back to face them and taking a sip of his drink, Harrolds said, "Normally I'd do what I've done all the years I've served my country, and feed you a load of shit. But I don't think I'll bother. Perhaps you're doing me a favor."

Booker, like a restless cat, had prowled over to peer into the kitchen, then had moved on to look through the bedroom door.

"There's no one else here, Major," Harrolds said.

"My wife and children had the good sense to go on about their own lives years ago. Do you have a family, Major?"

Booker gave him a bitter look, thinking of Margaret. "No. I had some plans, but they didn't work out."

Innocent of Booker's meaning, the older man said, "Well, perhaps you're fortunate."

Booker glowered at him, then realized the man had no idea that he had touched a nerve, and dismissed it.

Walking over to a window and staring down at the street three stories below, Harrolds said, "So this is what I get for having too much to drink and finding a sympathetic ear." He emitted an ironic laugh. "Can you imagine a career diplomat getting drunk and babbling at a Washington cocktail party? You don't get to *be* an old-timer here without learning not to do that."

He drained his glass and immediately went over to pour himself another drink. Turning to face Saunders and Booker again, he said, "Unless, of course, you're over the hill. An interesting phrase, 'over the hill.' Conrad Morgan's been telling me for years that that's where I am. A brilliant young man, Conrad. We all think we know what we want out of life. Conrad is one of those few who know how to get it. Of course he learned immediately of my drunken indiscretions. Capturing the indiscreet remark is a source of power in Washington, a lesson Conrad had learned well."

Smiling grimly, the prematurely aged man walked over to a table bearing a bowl of fruit and a paring knife. Picking up the knife, he examined his reflection in the shiny blade, then tossed it down again. "I may have been the one who first taught him that. Perhaps I am over the hill."

Booker and Saunders exchanged a look, a mixture of impatience and sympathy for the man.

"And she is a brilliant young woman," Harrolds continued. "And quite lovely. Something about her. I—I just wanted to talk to her. But, of course, you must know that by now, Major."

Booker gave the man an inquiring look.

Harrolds explained, "As leader of the Black Tigers, I assume she went directly to you. Otherwise you wouldn't be here. Morgan, of course, assumed the same thing. His efforts to find out what you knew and whom you might have told have probably kept you alive."

"The five men who came back with me weren't as lucky," Booker said bitterly.

Harrolds looked surprised. "All five so soon? It was to be expected eventually, of course, but so quickly bespeaks a rather frightening efficiency." After a short pause, he said, "My condolences would, of course, be meaningless."

Booker opened his mouth to make an angry rejoinder, but Saunders signaled him to silence. Staring down into his drink, Harrolds didn't notice.

In a reflective voice the Undersecretary of State said, "I was there in the beginning, when they invented the Phoenix Operation. You know what everyone got most upset about? Not the idea that we were consciously structuring a group of men whose purpose would be the clandestine murder of other men, nor the consequences that might befall us in another life for this decision based on political expediency. No. The thing that we got the most embroiled in was an argument over what a particular group of assassins we decided to call the Black Tigers—what that group of assassins would wear when they went out to relieve selected individuals of their very lives. Finally, after a great deal of bitter argument, we determined to dress the Black Tigers all in black. A commission was then paid to a noted designer, who shall remain nameless, who designed the black clothing that the Black Tigers wore when they rode out on their holy crusades."

He paused to take a sip of his drink. Booker and Saunders stared at him, both intrigued and impatient for him to get to the point.

"You made quite a reputation for yourselves," Harrolds said. "So great that the leaders of the North Vietnamese came to hate you with an all-consuming passion."

"We were set up," Booker said coldly.

"Oh, yes," Harrolds agreed.

"What was the deal?"

Harrolds sighed. "When I was a younger man, I knew I was going to be Secretary of State some day, perhaps even President. If I tell you the answer to that question, I may not even be afforded the opportunity of retiring next year with the modicum of dignity left to me."

Booker asked quietly, "Can you live with not telling me?"

Harrolds gave his head a resigned shake. "I suppose your life is not nearly so inconsequential to you as it is to Mr. Morgan, or even to me. Conrad made a deal with General Kuong Yin. The general had an obsession about the Black Tigers. He wanted you dead, all of you, and was willing to make large concessions if Conrad would give you to him. It was a matter of logistics. What were twelve lives in return for hundreds saved? Except to the twelve who were to be sacrificed, of course."

After a long silence, Saunders asked, "You have documentary proof of this?"

"Oh, yes. I'll show you a copy of the letter I wrote to four separate attorneys, with instructions to open it only upon my death. A form of life insurance, you might say. Conrad knows about the letters, but not who the attorneys are."

Going into the bedroom, Harrolds returned a moment later carrying a folded sheet of bond paper. He handed it to Saunders.

"You may keep this," he said. "I have several other copies."

24

As they walked out of the apartment building, Booker asked, "What's our next move? Taking the letter to the committee chairman?"

"You don't operate that way in Washington," Saunders said. "You'd be an outcast here. Nobody appreciates a scandal. The President would be embarrassed at appointing a scoundrel as Secretary of State, the committee would be embarrassed at treating him with kid gloves up to now, and no one would really like it except the gossip columnists."

"What then?" Booker asked.

"Our main goal is merely to stop this amoral monster from becoming Secretary of State, isn't it?"

"I guess," Booker agreed.

"So we'll stop him quietly, without scandal. We'll lay out to him what we have, and let him withdraw his nomination 'for reasons of health.' "

Boooker said dissatisfiedly, "That doesn't pay him back for Margaret."

"He probably didn't personally order that. Anyway, you can murder him at your leisure at some future time, if revenge is important to you. For the present, let's keep it civilized." He looked at his watch. "Four-thirty. Still time to catch him at work. One thing about top Washington bureaucrats: they put in long working days."

They walked up Pennsylvania Avenue until they found a public phone, and Saunders called the State Department. When he gave his name, he got through to Conrad Morgan almost immediately.

"How are you, Saunders?" the Secretary of State Designate said cordially. "Good to hear from you after all these years. Still with the CIA?"

Saunders said dryly, "You know I am, Mr. Morgan, or you wouldn't give me the time of day."

"You don't sound very friendly," Morgan said, his own voice still friendly.

"This isn't a social call," Saunders told him. "It's business. I'd like an appointment to discuss the Black Tigers."

"Oh?" Morgan said warily. "What about them?"

"I prefer to discuss it face-to-face. I've just come from Edgar Harrolds' place, Mr. Morgan."

There was a long period of silence before Morgan said, "I see. And?"

"I have a certain document that I can either discuss with you, or turn over to the Senate committee."

After another period of silence, Morgan said, "It's a bit late today because I'm going to a cocktail party at six. Suppose you come out to my house in the morning?"

"All right," Saunders agreed. "But this really

should be a private meeting. I don't think you'll want your family in on it."

"My family is away, visiting my wife's mother in Buffalo. We'll be quite alone, Saunders."

"Your address?"

"I have a call on another phone. I'll put my secretary back on to give you directions. It's a little complicated."

"All right," Saunders said. "What time in the morning?"

"Let's make it early," Morgan said. "Say eight o'clock. Here's my secretary."

The secretary came on to give Saunders directions to Conrad Morgan's home. Morgan didn't live in the District of Columbia, it developed, but in Maryland. As the Secretary of State Designate had said, the directions were a little complicated. They involved taking the Baltimore-Washington Parkway north, cutting west off of it on a minor, unnumbered road, then south again along another secondary road to an unmarked gravel road whose landmark was an old-fashioned, one-room red schoolhouse, and east along it.

When Saunders hung up and stepped from the phone booth, Booker said, "Well?"

"I called him Mr. Morgan, and he called me Saunders. I suppose it's better than being called Boy."

"What did he say," Booker asked patiently.

"We're to see him at his home, out in the boondocks, at eight in the morning. Which means we have to rent a hotel room for tonight, and a car in the morning."

"That's nice," Booker said. "Thanks a bunch for telling me we wouldn't be staying here long enough to need a razor and a change of clothes."

"We can pick some stuff up," Saunders told him. "Our immediate problem is to find a taxi."

A few minutes before 8:00 the next morning Saunders drove a rented Impala up the circular driveway of a country estate in Maryland. He parked in front of wide steps leading up to the pillared veranda of a white, two-story frame house. Saunders and Booker got out and mounted the steps.

"Why would this guy live halfway to Baltimore? Booker asked.

Saunders shrugged. "Who knows? Maybe it has something to do with Spiro Agnew."

"You must have influence," Booker said. "It wasn't very hard to get an appointment with the big man."

Pushing a doorbell, Saunders said, "I think he's very interested in what he thinks I might have to sell."

Musical chimes sounded from indoors. The door was opened by Morgan himself. He was wearing an expensive maroon smoking jacket over a pair of tailored slacks, and had leather slippers on his feet.

"No butler?" Saunders said.

"With the family away, I gave the servants time off too," Morgan said. "Good morning, Saunders. Please come in." Then he glanced questioningly at Booker. "I don't believe I know this gentleman."

"I am sure he will add to our discussion," Saunders said, moving past Morgan into the house.

"I see," Morgan said, not really seeing. When Booker had also moved past him into a wide entry hall and Morgan had closed the door, he said to Booker, "As I assume you know, I am Conrad Morgan."

"John T. Booker," Booker said tonelessly.

Morgan looked momentarily startled, but then his face became as expressionless as Booker's. Neither man offered his hand, nor said any of the common phrases acknowledging introduction.

"This way, please," Morgan said, leading the way across the entry hall through a wide front room furnished with Louis XIV furniture, and into a library fitted with a leather-covered sofa and several comfortable leather chairs. In one corner was a coffee service with a pot of coffee, cups, sugar and cream, and napkins on it.

"Please sit down, gentlemen," Morgan said. "Coffee?"

Both Booker and Saunders shook their heads. Morgan went over to pour himself a cup of coffee and add a spoon of sugar. Neither guest had accepted the offer of seats, and Morgan stood also.

He said, "Well, Saunders, I trust this rather unusual meeting is as important as you indicated. Something to do with the group once known as the Black Tigers, I believe you said."

"Something, yes," Saunders said. "Mr. Booker has a few questions."

Turning to Booker, Morgan said, "Well, can we get on with it? As I'm sure you may have heard, I have a rather busy day ahead."

"I'll try to be brief," Booker said. "Tell me if I've got the facts straight."

"Tell me the facts, and I'll do what I can."

"You made a secret deal at the Peace Talks with General Kuong Yin, the North Vietnamese negotiator."

Morgan sipped at his coffee. "Secret deals are the heart of diplomacy, Mr. Booker."

Booker said coldly, "This deal called for the murder of the Black Tigers."

Morgan hiked his eyebrows. "Murder, Mr. Booker?"

"Murder, Mr. Morgan," Booker confirmed. "One other American knows about it, and he talked."

"Indeed?" Morgan said with an air of unconcern, taking another sip of coffee.

Booker said, "At first I couldn't figure out why you didn't try to kill Harrolds along with the rest of us. He told me. He sent a registered letter to four lawyers, none of whom you know. The letters were to be opened in the event of his untimely death."

Still unconcerned, Morgan said, "Early Agatha Christie."

"And just as effective. The letters explained what was known between you and Kuong Yin as the Phoenix Solution. I also couldn't figure out what Major Mhin Van Thieu was doing, driving in and out of my life. At first I assumed he worked for 'them,' whoever 'they' were. But, of course, 'they' are you, and you are all one."

Morgan said sardonically, "We have met the enemy, and They are Us. Comic strip philosophy, Mr. Booker."

"Agreed," Booker said with a nod. "And now Kuong Yin is manipulating you like the comic strip diplomat you are. He waited patiently until the moment of your greatest vulnerability, the eve of your confirmation as Secretary of State. And now, with exquisite Oriental grace, he is blackmailing you into completing the deal you never finished: the extermination of the Black Tigers."

"They are very unforgiving people," Morgan said, still with no indication of concern.

"Toward you or the Black Tigers?"

"Toward Us, sir. We are Us."

"Perhaps," Booker said. "But now I think it's time to end the game."

He nodded toward Saunders, who had been enjoying the exchange with a slight smile on his face.

Reaching into his inside breast pocket, the black man drew out a folded letter.

Handing it to Morgan, he said, "You don't have to be careful with it, because there are lots of copies. But before you read it, Mr. Morgan, tell me something. Why do you address me as Saunders, and him as Mr. Booker?"

"Why because I regard you as a friend, Saunders," Morgan said easily. "Mr. Booker is as yet only an acquaintance."

25

There was silence while Conrad Morgan unfolded the letter and read it. Eventually he looked up with a slight smile on his face.

"An interesting document," he commented.

"Isn't it?" Booker agreed. He pointed to a phone on the library desk. "Now you're gonna pick up that phone and call the White House. Sudden personal problems are going to prevent you from accepting the nomination as Secretary of State."

Morgan's smile became condescending.

"If you don't, the news media are going to have one hell of a time with that letter."

Morgan said in a patronizing tone, "I understand, *Major* Booker, that you were quite a jungle fighter. But this is *my* kind of jungle, Major." He tossed the letter toward Booker, it landed on the floor between them, and neither man made any move to pick it up. "I'm afraid it just wouldn't be expedient for me to resign at this time."

"Expedient, huh?" Booker said. "Like it was expedient for you to send us on that POW raid."

Morgan gave his head an amused shake. "Expedience built America, Mr. Booker. It was expedient for this great democracy to have legal slavery for half of its existence. It was expedient to keep the vote from women for one hundred and fifty years. It was expedient to declare war on Mexico and oli. And it was expedient, goddamn it, to get rid of Montezuma, Major Booker, to the shores of Tripoli. And it was expedient, goddamm it, to get rid of the Black Tigers. A small price to pay for ending a war that was no longer expedient. How many Americans have given up their lives for lesser causes?"

The cynical logic touched a nerve in Booker, momentarily subduing him. Morgan pressed his advantage.

"It's really very simple, Mr. Booker. Despite all the empty rhetoric to the contrary, the end still justifies the means."

After considering this, Booker summoned a smile as cynical as Morgan's. "Like the seashore, Morgan?"

Morgan gave him a puzzled look.

Booker said, "It occurs to me that most of those who follow your logic end up in places like Elba or San Clemente."

Chuckling, Morgan said, "Come now, Booker."

"Does that mean we've become friends?" Booker asked sarcastically. "Check your history, Morgan. Most of our 'expedient' wars ended in failure. And our successes didn't just happen because they were expedient. Those Americans you spoke of gave up their lives *willingly*. Not exactly what you had in mind for the Black Tigers."

"Does that really make such a difference?"

"It makes *all* the difference, Morgan. People like you never do see that, and maybe they never will. It's not that you don't deserve to be Secretary of State. You don't deserve to live."

In the face of Booker's emotional outburst, Morgan still remained unruffled. Finishing the coffee in his cup, he carried the cup over to the service cart.

He started to say, "An interesting philosophy, Mr. Booker, but—" when Murray Saunders interrupted.

"But philosophy is bullshit, right, Morgan? Well, that letter isn't. So—"

Saunders pointed toward the phone. Morgan reached down to pick up the fallen letter and handed it to Booker.

"Here," he said. "Run over to the *Washington Post* with my best regards. But tell them they'll have a hard time verifying it with Harrolds. Visitors are not allowed in the Bethesda Hospital psychiatric ward."

Booker and Saunders looked at each other. Saunders went over to the table where the phone sat and began thumbing through the telephone book.

Morgan said to Booker, "They found him rolling on the floor and howling like a banshee. Took four men to get him into the straightjacket. A nervous disorder, they're calling it. But actually he's quite mad. A letter written by a madman isn't exactly what they call prime evidence, is it, Mr. Booker?"

Murray Saunders was saying into the phone, "I'd like to check on the condition of Mr. Edgar Harrolds."

After listening, he said, "Doing as well as can be expected isn't very informative, miss. I'm phoning from the home of Mr. Conrad Morgan. The Secretary Designate would like exact information as to his condition. Would you like me to put him on?"

After listening again, he said, "Thank you," and hung up.

Saunders gave Booker a rueful look that said Edgar Harrolds was as bad off as Morgan had suggested.

Morgan said briskly, "Well, gentlemen, as I've said, I have a big day." He started for the door from the library. "So, if you'll excuse me, I'm sure you can see yourselves out."

Because they had no other recourse, Booker and Saunders morosely followed Morgan through the front room and into the entry hall. Morgan continued on to the foot of the stairs leading to the second floor, but then halted and turned.

"Oh, by the way, Mr. Booker," he said. "Tragic news about your lady friend, Margaret Cash. I'm sure that all the research she had with her was irreplaceable. Tragic."

Booker started toward Morgan, but Saunders, who was between the two, put a restraining palm against his chest. After staring at Conrad Morgan for a moment, his face white with rage, Booker abruptly turned, jerked open the front door, and went out.

Saunders said to Morgan, "A diplomat is supposed to know enough to quit when he's ahead. You just came awfully close to getting yourself dead, Mr. Secretary Designate."

He followed Booker out.

A large black limousine was parked behind Saunders' rented Impala. The chauffeur, dressed formally in black, with a visored chauffeur's cap, was leaning against the side of the car. Booker might have paid no attention to him if he hadn't called it to himself by turning away the moment he spotted Booker, going around the car and slipping behind the wheel with his visor pulled down over his face. That made Booker change his course. He headed for the driver's side of the limousine. Reaching through the open window, he tilted the man's cap upward.

The chauffeur swiveled his head away so that Booker couldn't see his face. But Booker had already decided that he was the truck driver who had tried to push his Porsche out into traffic when Booker had Margaret in the car with him.

Booker said to the back of the man's head, "Is your accelerator pedal working all right today?"

"What the hell are you talking about?" the chauffeur muttered.

"You work for Morgan?"

The driver, with his face still averted, made no answer. Reaching into the car, Booker grabbed his chin and pulled his face around.

"Do you?" he asked, baring his teeth.

The man gazed at him apprehensively. "Listen, you got no right to push me around," he said with more fear than bravado in his voice.

Murray Saunders said from behind Booker, "What's the matter?"

Booker said, "This creep once tried to get me and Margaret killed in a traffic accident. Apparently he's Morgan's chauffeur."

Pulling open the door, Booker jerked the man from the car and slammed his back against the side of the car.

"Hey, take it easy," the chauffeur said plaintively, raising both hands palm out.

"What's your name?" Booker demanded.

"Franklin Jenner."

"Okay, Franklin Jenner, you're here to pick up Morgan, aren't you?"

The man nodded. "He said eight-thirty."

Booker glanced up at the house to see if Morgan was watching from a window. There was no sign of him.

"What time is it?" Booker asked Saunders.

"Eight-forty."

"We seem to have thrown off his schedule," Booker said.

Releasing his two-handed grip on the chauffeur's jacket, Booker slipped out of his suit coat and handed to to Saunders. To Jenner he said, "Get off that jacket and cap."

"What?" the man said without understanding.

Booker said with deadly impatience, "You have a choice. You may hand me your jacket and cap, or I'll take them off your unconscious body. If you haven't made a decision within the next three seconds, I'll make it for you."

Hurriedly the chauffeur took off his jacket and cap and handed them to Booker. After another glance at the house, Booker put them on. They didn't fit perfectly, but they were adequate.

Getting behind the wheel of the limousine, Booker said to Saunders, "Why don't you take Mr. Franklin Jenner somewhere far away?"

"Be a pleasure," Saunders said. He gave the chauffeur a poke in the ribs and pointed toward the Impala. "Move, Mr. Franklin Jenner."

The man obediently went over to the Impala. But when Saunders opened the front door on the passenger side for him to get in, he just stood there.

Regarding Saunders estimatingly, he said, "I don't know why I should follow your orders. I think I could take you."

Saunders gave him a delighted smile. "Okay, start off."

The chauffeur's expression became uncertain. "On the other hand, why should I maybe break a knuckle over something that's none of my business?"

He got into the car. Looking disappointed, Saunders rounded to the driver's side, tossed Booker's suit coat into the back seat and slid behind the wheel. There was dead silence as he drove along the gravel road until it came out on the secondary road. Saunders turned left there, drove on until he came to a driveway where he could turn around, then came back to park on the shoulder about a quarter block back from the gravel road.

"Who are you?" Franklin Jenner asked.

Saunders took out the fake ID that identified him as an FBI agent and handed it over. After examining it, Jenner handed it back.

"That other guy's not FBI," he said. "He's an instructor at UCLA named John T. Booker."

"Yes," Saunders agreed. "And the target of a murder conspiracy of which you're a part."

"That thing he was talking about was an accident," the man protested. "My gas pedal stuck."

"Coincidental that you just happened to be there, wasn't it?" Saunders said sarcastically. "Where was this, by the way?"

"Los Angeles," Jenner said sullenly.

"You were clear across the country when your gas pedal stuck. And you just happened to be behind Booker. You know who he is and where he works. Yet it was all an accident."

For several seconds the chauffeur was silent. Then he asked sullenly, "Am I under arrest?"

"We're after bigger game," Saunders said. "Just sit still and shut up."

Five minutes passed in silence. Then the black limousine turned off the gravel road a quarter block away, swung right, and moved away from them.

Reaching across Jenner to open the door, Saunders said, "Here's where you get out."

The man climbed from the car, closed the door and stood looking in at the black man.

Smiling from the teeth out, Saunders said, "Now you can get to a phone and start making calls, or you can forget you ever worked for Conrad Morgan and hit the road out of town. In the former case I'll be back for you with a warrant for conspiracy to commit murder. In the latter you're home free."

"I'll get out of town," Jenner said.

"You're smarter than you look," Saunders told him, and drove off in pursuit of the limousine.

26

As Murray Saunders drove off in the Impala with Conrad Morgan's chauffeur, Booker examined the interior of the limousine. The rear section was a rolling living room. There was a well-stocked bar with a small counter that slid out from a recess. It was pulled out, and a crystal goblet of red wine stood on it, presumably poured by the chauffeur as a regular morning chore. A fifteen-inch TV set was built into the dividing partition between the rear area and the driver's compartment. A thick plexiglass window sealed off the rear section from the front seat, but there was a speaker device so that passengers could converse with the driver.

With tools from the trunk, Booker removed both rear inner door handles.

It was another five minutes after the Impala drove off before the Secretary of State Designate appeared from the house. Booker turned to gaze toward the road, so that the back of his head would be to Morgan as he got into the rear seat. As soon as he was in, Booker faced forward again.

Pressing a button below the built-in speaker, Morgan said, "We're running a little late, Franklin. This morning you had better forget the speed limit."

The chauffeur waved acknowledgment without turning around. As the limousine glided off, Morgan turned on the TV set and settled back to watch the news. It was already on. A newscaster was seated at the desk, talking, and behind him was a large picture of Morgan. The newscaster was saying:

> . . . *and also making an appearance at the White House today will be Conrad Morgan, who will be sworn in later this morning as the nation's new Secretary of State.*

Morgan gazed at his own picture contentedly, savoring the moment. The newcomer continued:

> *Morgan, one of the youngest men ever to achieve this high office, is described as one of the new breed of diplomats for the seventies. Well, in Chicago today, the windy city really . . .*

Morgan reached forward to switch off the TV set. He took an appreciative sip of wine, set down the glass, and glanced out the window. He frowned when he saw unfamiliar country rolling by. He looked out the other side, through the rear window, and ahead. Then he pressed the speaker button.

"Where are you going, Franklin?" he asked.

There was no answer from the chauffeur. Peering at him through the dividing glass, Morgan suddenly realized by the size of the man's shoulders that he was not Franklin Jenner.

"What the hell is this?" he said angrily. "Who——"

He abruptly cut it off when Booker turned his head to grin at him through the glass. His voice came through the intercom, saying cheerily, "Good morning, Mr. Secretary."

For a moment Morgan was startled into speechlessness. Then he shouted, "Booker! Just what the hell do you think you're doing?"

"You said I was a good jungle fighter," Booker said, still cheerily. "I'm also a fast learner."

Morgan leaned forward to slide open the plexiglass window. It was tightly locked from the other side.

"Stop this car, you crazy fool!" he yelled.

Booker merely accelerated to a higher speed. Morgan reached for the door handle on the right, saw it was missing and reached for the one on the left. It was missing too.

"What do you want, Booker?" Morgan asked with a touch of panic in his voice. "What do you expect to accomplish by this nonsense?"

"Relax, Morgan," Booker said. "We're just going to talk."

Having no option, Morgan decided to humor the madman. "All right. About what?"

"There's a news documentary about your life scheduled on Channel Two about now," Booker said. "Why don't we listen to that while we talk?"

Morgan reached forward to turn on the set and switch it to Channel Two. The program had already started. On the screen there was a five-year-old newsfilm running, showing Morgan talking to reporters in Paris. The newscaster's voice was saying:

> . . . *and Morgan's role in the talks was credited with the saving of thousands of lives, both American and Vietnamese. After returning from the talks, Morgan played a major role in discussions between the Israeli government and leaders of the Palestinian refugees. His talent for high-level negotiations made him one of the few State Department leaders to retain his high position through three national administrations.*

Booker's voice came through the intercom, cutting above the voice of the newscaster. "What you said about expedience made a hell of a lot of sense, Morgan. I see there's only one way to deal with people like you: expediently. You've won all the battles, but you're going to lose the war. How'd you like to be an MIA? Huh? Missing in action."

Switching off the TV set, Morgan asked, "What are you talking about?"

"When it comes time for your swearing in today, you aren't gonna be there."

Morgan looked around uneasily. They were now traveling at a breathtaking speed that would have been frightening even if the car wasn't being driven by a maniac.

He said without any great assurance, "I'll be there."

Booker's head moved back and forth. "No way."

"You're dreaming," Morgan said.

"Am I?" Booker asked, pressing down on the accelerator to put the big car at an even more frightening speed.

Looking straight ahead so that he couldn't see how fast the landscape was moving alongside of them, Morgan said with feigned amusement that failed to cover the tremor in his voice, "They're going to come looking for me, Booker. You just can't disappear with a Secretary of State without arousing someone's ire."

"Let 'em look."

"All right, Booker," Morgan said with a touch of desperation. "What's your plan?"

Booker said, "If you get away with this, Morgan, it's betrayal of every guy who died in any war we ever had. And God knows how many more people you'll kill in the future. I'm not gonna let it happen."

"You're insane, Booker," Morgan said in a high voice. "This won't work."

"You can bet your sweet ass it will," Booker's voice came from the intercom.

Morgan lost control. "You're crazy, you goddamn idiot!" he screamed. "Now stop this car or I'm going to kill you!"

There was no response from the driver. Morgan reached under the bar counter for a heavy wine decanter and held it up threateningly to the glass behind Booker's head. Glancing in the rear-view mirror, Booker saw the raised decanter. His only reaction was to increase the headlong speed even more.

"I'll do it!" Morgan screamed. "I'll kill you!"

"You're panicking, Morgan," Booker said mockingly.

They started over a bridge spanning Chesapeake Bay. Behind Booker there was a crash as Morgan smashed the dividing glass with the heavy decanter. There was a shower of glass fragments, then Morgan's left arm went about Booker's neck in a stranglehold.

"Stop the car, Booker!" he shouted.

With his head pulled so far backward that all he could see was the roof of the car, Booker lost control. The limousine burst through the bridge's guard rail and arced through the air toward the water below.

Releasing his grip around Booker's neck, Morgan screamed, "Bookerrrrr—"

Booker pushed the door open on the driver's side and dived from the car an instant before it hit the water. With a huge splash the limousine disappeared and plunged to the bottom of the bay.

Booker's dive was as shallow as he could make it. He came up several yards from where the car had gone down and looked back, treading water. A huge bubble rose to the surface and burst.

He was about a hundred yards from shore. Swimming to shore, he climbed from the water and again looked back. Smaller bubbles were now rising from the spot where the car had gone down. Cars passed from either direction, but the occupants failed to notice the bubbles.

Booker became conscious of a stinging sensation at the side of his head and put his hand up to feel. It came away bloody. There was a small gash there from a piece of the flying glass.

Turning, he climbed the bank to the crossroad intersecting the main road over the bridge. It was a narrow gravel road, completely trafficless. But as he started toward the bridge, a single car turned off of the main road onto it.

Murray Saunders pulled the Impala over next to the drenched, bleeding, exhausted Booker. He looked at Booker for a moment, then at the bubbles still rising from the submerged car.

"The last casualty of the Vietnam War," he said.

Booker leaned against the car, avoiding looking at the water. "The end of the tunnel," he said. "Why can't I feel anything but disgust? For him, and for myself."

Saunders said, "We have met the enemy, and they are us."

Sighing, Booker nodded his head in silent agreement.

"Give you a lift?" Saunders invited.

Booker slowly got into the car next to him.

"Try not to drip on me," Saunders said as they drove off. "This is the only suit I have with me."

Booker looked at him. The one he was wearing was the only one he had with him, too. But at the moment it didn't seem important.

More Movie Tie-ins from SIGNET

☐ **THE BINGO LONG TRAVELING ALL-STARS AND MOTOR KINGS** by William Brashler. (#W6833—$1.50)

☐ **THE DOMINO PRINCIPLE** by Adam Kennedy. (#J7389—$1.95)

☐ **DIRTY HANDS** by Richard Neely. (#W7381—$1.50)

☐ **THE ISLAND OF DR. MOREAU** by H. G. Wells. (#Y7495—$1.25)

☐ **THE INCREDIBLE SARAH** by Alan Arnold. (#W7215—$1.50)

☐ **JOSEPH ANDREWS** by Henry Fielding. (#Y7379—$1.25)

☐ **LIES MY FATHER TOLD ME** by Norman Allan. (#W6783—$1.50)

☐ **THE MAN WITH THE GOLDEN GUN** by Ian Fleming. (#Y6208—$1.25)

☐ **A MATTER OF TIME** by Maurice Druon. (#W7175—$1.50)

☐ **THE OLD CURIOSITY SHOP** as **MR. QUILP** by Charles Dickens. (#Y6420—$1.25)

☐ **THE OMEN** by David Seltzer. (#W7065—$1.50)

☐ **PAPER MOON** by Joe David Brown. (#W7448—$1.50)

☐ **ROYAL FLASH** by George MacDonald Fraser. (#W6748—$1.50)

☐ **2001: A SPACE ODYSSEY** by Arthur C. Clarke. (#J7765—$1.95)

☐ **WHITE LINE FEVER** by C. S. Cotelo. (#W6701—$1.50)

Big Bestsellers from SIGNET

☐ **HOW TO SAVE YOUR OWN LIFE** by Erica Jong.
(#E7959—$2.50)

☐ **WHITEY AND MICKEY** by Whitey Ford, Mickey Mantle, and Joseph Durso. (#J7963—$1.95)

☐ **MISTRESS OF DESIRE** by Rochelle Larkin.
(#E7964—$2.25)

☐ **THE QUEEN AND THE GYPSY** by Constance Heaven.
(#J7965—$1.95)

☐ **TORCH SONG** by Anne Roiphe. (#J7901—$1.95)

☐ **OPERATION URANIUM SHIP** by Dennis Eisenberg, Eli Landau and Menahem Portugale. (#E8001—$1.75)

☐ **NIXON VS. NIXON** by Dr. David Abrahamsen.
(#E7902—$2.25)

☐ **ISLAND OF THE WINDS** by Athena Dallas-Damis.
(#J7905—$1.95)

☐ **CARRIE** by Stephen King. (#J7280—$1.95)

☐ **'SALEM'S LOT** by Stephen King. (#E8000—$2.25)

☐ **THE SHINING** by Stephen King. (#E7872—$2.50)

☐ **SLEEP POSITIONS: The Night Language of the Body** by Dr. Samuel Dunkell. (#E7875—$2.25)

☐ **OAKHURST** by Walter Reed Johnson. (#J7874—$1.95)

☐ **FRENCH KISS** by Mark Logan. (#J7876—$1.95)

☐ **COMA** by Robin Cook. (#E7881—$2.50)

THE NEW AMERICAN LIBRARY, INC.,
P.O. Box 999, Bergenfield, New Jersey 07621

Please send me the SIGNET BOOKS I have checked above. I am enclosing $_____(check or money order—no currency or C.O.D.'s). Please include the list price plus 35¢ a copy to cover handling and mailing costs. (Prices and numbers are subject to change without notice.)

Name_____

Address_____

City_____State_____Zip Code_____
Allow at least 4 weeks for delivery

More Big Bestsellers from SIGNET

☐ **THE YEAR OF THE INTERN by Robin Cook.**
(#E7881—$2.50)

☐ **MISTRESS OF DARKNESS by Christopher Nicole.**
(#J7782—$1.95)

☐ **SOHO SQUARE by Clare Rayner.** (#J7783—$1.95)

☐ **CALDO LARGO by Earl Thompson.** (#E7737—$2.25)

☐ **A GARDEN OF SAND by Earl Thompson.**
(#E8039—$2.50)

☐ **TATTOO by Earl Thompson.** (#E8038—$2.50)

☐ **DESIRES OF THY HEART by Joan Carroll Cruz.**
(#J7738—$1.95)

☐ **THE ACCURSED by Paul Boorstin.** (#E7745—$1.75)

☐ **RUNNING AWAY by Charlotte Vale Allen.**
(#E7740—$1.75)

☐ **THE RICH ARE WITH YOU ALWAYS by Malcolm Macdonald.**
(#E7682—$2.25)

☐ **THE WORLD FROM ROUGH STONES by Malcolm Macdonald.**
(#J6891—$1.95)

☐ **THE FRENCH BRIDE by Evelyn Anthony.**
(#J7683—$1.95)

☐ **TELL ME EVERYTHING by Marie Brenner.**
(#J7685—$1.95)

☐ **ALYX by Lolah Burford.** (#J7640—$1.95)

☐ **MACLYON by Lolah Burford.** (#J7773—$1.95)

THE NEW AMERICAN LIBRARY, INC.,
P.O. Box 999, Bergenfield, New Jersey 07621

Please send me the SIGNET BOOKS I have checked above. I am enclosing $_____(check or money order—no currency or C.O.D.'s). Please include the list price plus 35¢ a copy to cover handling and mailing costs. (Prices and numbers are subject to change without notice.)

Name_____

Address_____

City_____State_____Zip Code_____
Allow at least 4 weeks for delivery